Charli Grey

GLITTER
BATON

Glitter Baton by Charli Grey

Printed in the United States of America
First Printing, August 2025
ISBN: 978-1968178246

Ink and Revival Publishing
Virginia, USA

For the ones who've been discarded, silenced, or shamed—
You are not what they did to you.
You are not what you lost.
You are what you survived.

This is for the woman who made it out with nothing
but her breath,
for the girl who held her pain in silence because
speaking it felt too dangerous,
and for the warrior who still wakes up each day
choosing healing,
even when the world offers no map.

May this story remind you:
Your truth is holy.
Your scars are sacred.
And your survival is a testimony.

You didn't break.
You became.

Table of Contents

PROLOGUE

Survivors Convention – Dallas, Texas

The mic was warm in my hand—like it had been waiting for me.

The room was quiet, but not empty.

No, it was full—full of stories.

Stories that looked just like mine.

Stories no one had ever dared to write down.

I stood still for a moment and let the silence settle. That kind of stillness feels like a reckoning. You can hear your heartbeat in your ears. You can feel the tension in the room like a wire stretched too tight. You know you're about to say something that might just rearrange someone's life.

"Good afternoon," I began. "My name is Ruth. And before anything else—before the titles, before the healing, before the forgiveness—I was broken."

A few heads bowed. A few eyes locked on mine.

That's how you know you're in a room full of women who get it.

They don't flinch when you say broken.

They've been living with that word stitched into their skin like a second name.

"I didn't come here to tell you I'm healed," I continued. "I came to tell you I'm healing. Present tense. Still. And that healing... looks nothing like I thought it would."

I saw someone wipe her eyes with the sleeve of her sweatshirt. Another one sat stiff, arms crossed, but her foot was bouncing. She heard me. Even if she wasn't ready to admit it.

"People talk about survival like it's a light switch. On or

off. Alive or gone. But trauma doesn't play fair like that. It lives in the shadows of your choices, in the tone of your voice, in the panic of waking up when nothing is even wrong. It shows up in the middle of joy, just to remind you it's still there."

I paced slowly across the stage. "Some of us carry trauma like a scream trapped in the chest. Others—like a whisper under the skin. Either way, your body keeps score. It remembers what your mind tries to forget. And eventually... it demands your attention."

A woman in the back nodded so hard, her earrings rattled.

"You can move to a new city, change your name, find Jesus, get married, cut your hair, go vegan, speak in tongues, journal, detox, and tell yourself you're over it. But if you haven't faced it, your body will remind you."

The room was still again. This time, not from discomfort—but reverence.

"I've crossed cities, states, and countries trying to outrun my pain. But it followed me. Sometimes quietly, sometimes loud. I built whole lives around silence, around secrets. But silence is not the same as safety. It's just slower drowning."

I paused. Let the weight sit.

"I'm not standing here because I got it all right. I'm

standing here because I didn't let what happened to me be the final word. I chose to become more than the worst thing I survived. And if you're here today, you can too."

I gripped the mic a little tighter.

"You don't have to know how. You don't have to feel ready. You just have to want more than the numbness. Want something that feels like hope. Want to live like you deserve peace, even if you don't believe it yet."

And then I said the words I always say, not because I rehearsed them, but because they're true:

"You are not crazy. You are not too much. And you are not to blame."

I took a breath and looked out across the women—some older, some barely grown, some mothers, some mourning.

"This is not a testimony of perfection. This is a testimony of survival. Of grace. Of starting over again and again until starting over becomes your superpower. I stand before you now not just as a survivor, but as a witness—of pain, of healing, of redemption. But I didn't arrive here overnight. There was a long road, paved with confusion, betrayal, manipulation, and loss. And if you'll allow me, I want to walk you through that journey—not because it's easy to remember, but because it's necessary to tell.

There are pieces of myself I left scattered across years and cities. But I found my way back. Piece by piece. "

Then I smiled, the kind of smile that costs something, and said:

"This is how it happened. This is how I became."

CHAPTER 1

The Red Duffel Bag

"The wound is the place where the Light enters you."
— Rumi

"You Just Don't Wanna Know"
– Marvin Winans

I didn't pack much.

Just a red duffel bag with one working zipper, a few shirts, and a single can of corn. That was all I had—well, that and a truth too heavy to keep carrying.

The day I left home wasn't loud. No screaming. No fights. Just air too thick to breathe and silence that knew too much.

My sister had called her boyfriend to come get me. I needed a ride home. That's all. But instead of heading toward my street, he kept driving. Past the gas station. Past the turnoff. Past the last place I knew how to scream.

What happened next—what he took—stayed on me like smoke. A stink I couldn't scrub off no matter how long I stood in a hot shower. And I stood in a few. God knows I did. But nothing washed away the weight of being violated in a loft above some hidden apartment like I was nothing.

So one day, I chose something. Anything. I packed what I had, grabbed my stash of single bills, and boarded a Greyhound headed toward Houston with no destination except "not here."

Nobody at the terminal noticed me. That's the funny thing about girls who've been hurt—we're easy to ignore when we stop trying to be seen.

I clutched the red duffel like it could answer prayers, staring down the long stretch of seats and city lights. Every bump in the road felt like a memory. Every exit we passed reminded me I was finally leaving something behind... even if I didn't know what was waiting ahead.

I tried asking around when I got to Houston. Friends. Sort-of-friends. Strangers who used to laugh with me back when life didn't hurt like this. I got doors closed in my face and cold shoulders that didn't even flinch. Nobody wanted a girl with a bag full of shame and a can of corn.

I ended up back at Greyhound.

Sat there overnight. Slept on a plastic chair, back crooked and knees tucked up to my chest, like I could make myself small enough to disappear. Nobody bothered me. Nobody asked if I was okay. I wasn't.

The vending machine flickered like it was mourning, too. I had fifty-seven cents and a can of corn in my duffel. That was it. Not enough for a soda. Not enough for a plan. I chewed a piece of gum I found in my coat pocket and tried to think clearly, but the buzz of fear in my ears made it hard to hear myself.

I called one of my old friends from a pay phone. She picked up, laughed like it was nothing, and told me her mama didn't want "runaways or trouble" in their house. She hung up before I could respond.

I called another. No answer.

And another. Straight to voicemail.

I stopped calling after that. You learn pretty quickly who believes you—and who believes what's easier to believe.

I spent the next two nights floating.

One night in a stranger's car—someone who "felt bad"

for me and let me sleep in the back seat in exchange for promises I didn't keep. One night in a laundromat that stayed open 24 hours. I pretended to fold things that weren't mine, pretending I was waiting for someone who wasn't coming.

By the third night, I knew I couldn't keep pretending.

My body was stiff. My brain felt foggy. That's what trauma does—it moves in, shuts the lights off, and whispers that maybe this is all you'll ever be.

But I kept walking.

Until I passed a big glass door with a crooked sign taped inside:

COVENANT HOUSE.

If you're tired, come inside.

The woman at the desk didn't ask me to explain myself.

She just looked me in the eye and said, "You hungry?"

I nodded. My throat burned. I hadn't realized I was crying until I tasted salt on my lip.

They gave me a tray. Something warm. A juice box. I ate slowly, like I had to earn it. Then they took my name, my bag, and what was left of my trust.

I was shown to a bunk bed in a shared room with three other girls. One of them snored. One of them prayed out loud before she slept. One of them stared at the ceiling like it was the only place she could look without breaking.

Nobody asked questions that night. That was the rule. You don't ask, and you don't have to answer. Not unless you're ready.

I wasn't.

But I laid down, pulled the thin blanket over my shoulders, and closed my eyes.

That night, for the first time in a long time, I didn't dream about being chased.

I dreamed about standing still.

The next morning, I woke to the sound of metal clinking.

Somebody was folding a cot nearby, dragging it across the tile like it owed them something. My back ached from the too-thin mattress. My knees were sore from curling into myself all night. For a moment, I didn't know where I was. The hum of fluorescent lights overhead, the faint scent of bleach and burnt coffee, the soft shuffle of slippers on linoleum—it wasn't until I heard a girl humming a gospel song under her breath that it came back to me.

Covenant House.

I was still here.

I sat up slowly, blinking against the light. The bunk above mine creaked as someone shifted. A faded bulletin board on the wall had flyers about GED classes and free HIV testing. Another girl brushed her teeth in the open doorway of the shared bathroom, spitting into a sink with a sigh that sounded heavier than it should've.

Someone had left a pair of socks rolled neatly at the foot of my bed. Not mine. I stared at them like they were a puzzle.

A soft knock came at the doorframe. I turned my head too fast and winced.

"Good morning," the woman said, gently. She was maybe mid-forties, round face, warm brown eyes behind big glasses. No badge, no clipboard—just a denim button-down and a cross necklace that looked like it'd been through something. "I'm Miss Cora. You must be Ruth." I hesitated. I wasn't used to hearing my name said without judgment.

"I know you just got in last night," she said. "Would you be willing to come sit with me for a bit? No pressure, just breakfast and a quiet room."

I nodded without really meaning to. My throat still burned. My stomach felt like it didn't know if it should be hungry or shut down.

I followed her down the hallway. The floor tiles were mismatched in places, patched like skin over old wounds. Posters lined the walls—some peeling at the corners, others laminated and shining. *You Are More Than What Happened To You. Hope Lives Here.*

The dining area was smaller than I expected. Maybe four plastic tables, each with a napkin dispenser and a few chipped coffee mugs stacked to the side. A radio played faintly in the background—an old R&B song that made me ache for something I couldn't name.

I sat across from her, hands in my lap, while she poured me a paper cup of orange juice.

"Here," she said, sliding a plate toward me. Scrambled eggs. A biscuit. Two slices of bacon. "We do what we can with what we have." It smelled like salt and grease and warmth.

"Thank you," I whispered.

We ate in silence for a while. I didn't trust her yet, but I also didn't feel like she was waiting for me to fall apart.

When I'd finished, she offered me another juice and leaned back in her chair.

"We don't ask you to explain anything," she said. "Not until you're ready. Sometimes not even then. You don't owe us a play-by-play."

I looked down at the fork I was still holding. My knuckles were white.

"But if you want help," she continued, "we'll need your voice. Even if it's shaky. Even if it's just a whisper."

My throat tightened.

I wanted to say something. But the words felt too big for my mouth.

She didn't press. Just pulled a soft, green notebook from her canvas tote and set it in front of me. "This is yours. You don't have to write anything deep. You can write your grocery list if you want. But I've seen girls stitch their whole soul back together in a notebook like this. One sentence at a time."

I ran my fingers across the cover. It wasn't new—maybe leftover from a donation box—but it was clean. The edges were still sharp.

Miss Cora stood up. "There's a group meeting this afternoon. Optional. If you want to come, you can just sit and listen."

I nodded again. My voice still hadn't found me.

As she left the room, she paused at the door.

"You're not alone, Ruth. You're not the first girl to walk in with a bag full of broken pieces. And you're not the first who didn't want to tell anybody what happened." She smiled, not with pity, but with something closer to recognition.

"I just wanted you to know—we see you. Even if you're not ready to be seen."

She left me sitting at that table with an empty plate and a notebook I didn't know how to use.

But I opened it.

And on the first line, I wrote:

"I'm still here."

CHAPTER 2

Covenant & Survival

"Faith is taking the first step even when you don't see the whole staircase."
— Martin Luther King, Jr.

"The Battle Is Not Yours"
– Yolanda Adams

I didn't trust routine. Not yet.

Routine had never meant safety for me—just the slow countdown to when everything would fall apart again.

But somehow, Covenant House snuck rhythm into my body before I realized I was keeping time.

Wake up. Brush teeth. Eat.
Talk if you want.
Don't if you can't.
And every night—

A bed. A real one.

Three days passed before I noticed I hadn't flinched in my sleep.

I moved slow, more out of protection than fatigue. I watched everyone. Took notes in my head about who sobbed when they thought nobody could hear, who laughed too hard like they were trying to scare the silence, and who walked through the halls like they were made of glass.

Nobody asked me why I was there. And I didn't ask them either. It felt like we all knew—your story was yours, and it wasn't owed to anyone.

Miss Cora showed up every morning like clockwork. Sometimes she brought a muffin. Sometimes she just gave me a nod. She never pressed, never hovered. She had a way of letting you feel seen without feeling watched. I didn't know how to receive that. I wasn't used to gentle.

I'd started writing in that green notebook she gave me. Not much. Just bits and pieces:

"Slept through the night."
"Girl in the blue robe gave me her extra crackers."
"Still can't look in mirrors too long."

One morning, after roll call and lights-on, Miss Cora called my name. "Ruth? Can I borrow you for a second?"

Borrow me.

It was such a soft way to ask. I stood up and followed her, nervous anyway. That's the thing about trauma—you flinch even when it's kindness calling your name.

We walked past the case worker offices, past a bulletin board filled with laminated quotes and Bible verses. I noticed one curling at the edges: *"For I know the plans I have for you..."* I looked away before I could finish reading it.

She brought me into a small room with a table and two chairs. The walls were painted a pale yellow, like someone thought color alone could warm a place. She handed me a packet.

"You've been here about a week," she said. "And the staff thinks you're a strong fit for Rights of Passage."

I looked down at the paper in my hands. It mentioned housing, structure, mentoring. A dorm-style place across town with a little more freedom—and more responsibility.

"So... is this like... am I being moved?"

"It's not a punishment," she said quickly. "It's an opportunity. One we think you're ready for."

Ready. That word landed funny in my chest.

I hadn't been called ready in a long time. I'd been called dramatic. Difficult. Damaged. But never ready.

"You don't have to decide today," she added. "But I think you know when it's time to take the next step... even if you can't see where it's leading."
Her eyes didn't waver when she said it.

She meant it.

She believed in me in a way I hadn't even decided to believe in myself yet.

The next morning, I packed the red duffel again.

Only this time, I wasn't running. I folded each shirt like it mattered. I zipped the bag without trembling. The can of corn was gone. In its place, the green notebook and a fresh pair of socks I didn't remember earning.

I didn't know what *Rights of Passage* would hold. Didn't know who I'd be when I got there. But I was still here. And that had to mean something.

I didn't say goodbye.

Not because I didn't care—but because I didn't know how. What do you say to girls who've shared your toothpaste, your nightmares, your silence? Girls who cried just loud enough at night to wake you, but never loud enough to ask for help?

Word had gotten around by the time I zipped the duffel.

A few younger girls kept glancing at me sideways, their whispers soft but sharp. Jealousy hangs in the air different when it's coming from the broken. It's not petty—it's fear. Fear that someone else is leaving while they're still stuck.

I understood it. I'd felt it, once.

One of the older women sat on the edge of her bed, staring through me like I was already gone. Her eyes didn't blink when I passed her. She didn't say a word. I wondered how long she'd been there. How many people she'd watched come and go. How many times she told herself next time would be hers.

Miss Cora found me near the exit. She had a manila folder in one hand and a granola bar in the other.

"For the road," she said. "And the paperwork you'll need."

I nodded. I couldn't speak. My throat was too full of everything I hadn't processed yet.

"You're ready, Ruth," she said gently, resting a hand on my shoulder. "You don't have to believe it yet—I'll believe it for you."

Then she gave me a Metro bus map, a single fare token, and a blessing I wasn't sure I deserved.

The ride across town was chaos.

The bus was packed. School kids. Grocery bags. A man arguing with someone invisible to the rest of us. I sat near the back, duffel pressed into my lap like armor, eyes locked on a window too smudged to see through.

I hated how loud it was.
I hated how quiet I felt.

The driver missed my stop the first time. I had to yank the cord twice before he finally grumbled and pulled over. I stepped off the bus into a part of the city I didn't recognize—gray buildings, cracked sidewalks, the smell of hot concrete and diesel fumes. No one waited for me. No one waved.

I stood there for a minute, pretending I knew where I was going.

I checked the map three times. Walked two blocks the wrong direction. Doubled back. Nearly gave up when I couldn't find the street sign that matched the one Miss Cora had circled in pink.

By the time I found the building, my shirt was soaked with sweat. My legs ached. My stomach was tight with nerves.

It didn't look like much—just a long beige structure with two rusted doors and a faded mural on the side: a set of wings, barely visible, painted over bricks.

I stood outside for a moment, catching my breath.
Then I did something I hadn't done in a long time.

I prayed.

Not loud. Not poetic. Just a whisper in my chest:

"God, please. Let this be different."

And then, I reached for the handle.

The building smelled like Pine-Sol and something faintly burned—like toast left too long in a shared kitchen. The lobby was small and square, with two faded chairs on one side and a corkboard overflowing with flyers, half of them torn or curling at the corners.

There was no welcome sign. No flowers. No one waiting with open arms. Just a woman at a desk with short, pressed hair and a sharp face that didn't smile when I walked in.

"You must be Ruth," she said, flipping through a folder without looking up.

I nodded, then remembered to speak. "Yes, ma'am."

"ID?"

"I don't have one."
She glanced at me, then back at the folder. "Covenant called. You're cleared. I'll need you to sign these." She slid a clipboard toward me. "Rules. Curfew. Chore assignments. Room key's at the bottom."

I took the pen. My hand trembled slightly. She noticed, but didn't mention it.

"You'll be in Unit B. Second floor. Bathroom's at the end of the hall. Breakfast is at seven. Group check-in at six sharp every night. Lights out at ten. No guests. No substances. No exceptions."

Her voice was flat, not cruel—just practiced. Like she'd said it a hundred times and expected to say it a hundred more. There wasn't warmth, but there wasn't judgment either.

I signed everything. I didn't read the fine print.

She handed me a key attached to a neon green tag. "Room 208. Top bunk's free."

Then she turned back to her computer like I wasn't there.

I stood still for a second too long.

"You can go now," she added, not unkindly—just efficiently.

So I did.

The hallway leading to Unit B was dim and too quiet. I

heard a vacuum humming somewhere behind a closed door and the low thud of footsteps above me. The stairwell creaked as I climbed. Each step felt like it might give out, but didn't.

Room 208 was halfway down the hall. The door was chipped at the bottom. Someone had scratched a name into the paint: **Kia**. I wondered if Kia still lived here or if she'd made it out.

Inside, the room held two beds, two small dressers, and a cracked mirror hanging above a tiny sink. The walls were yellowing at the corners. One side was covered in magazine cutouts—quotes, celebrities, a photo of Whitney Houston with the words *"flawless"* written in Sharpie.

My new roommate wasn't there.

The top bunk had no sheets, just a bare mattress and a thin pillow. A folded towel sat on the edge like a peace offering.

I dropped the duffel and sat on the bottom step of the bunk, unsure whether I should unpack or pretend I hadn't arrived yet.

Outside the window, I could hear kids yelling in the alley. A dog barked. Somewhere, someone was playing gospel music too loud. I closed my eyes and let the sound wash over me.

I was here.
I had made it across town.
I had a bed.
A key.

And rules that didn't involve surviving someone else's anger.

The mirror in this room is cracked, and I haven't looked in it yet.

Not on purpose.

I know what I look like.
Tired.
Skin dry.
Braids loose at the edges.
That empty look people get when they stop trying to explain why they're sad.

I'm not trying to impress anybody here. That feels like another lifetime.

I waited until the hallway was quiet before I pulled out the green notebook again. Crawled up onto the top bunk and opened it like it was a Bible—slow, careful, hoping it still had something to say.

Day One at Rights of Passage

This place is too quiet. It makes my thoughts louder. I miss noise I can predict.

I'm not sure what I'm supposed to feel. Grateful? Safe? I feel... floaty. Like I'm in someone else's life and they forgot to tell me what page we're on.

I still haven't called my mama.

Not because I don't care—but because I don't know what I'd say.

"Hi Ma, remember when I walked out of the house with five dollars and a can of corn? I wasn't being dramatic—I just couldn't breathe. The air in that house was too thick. The silence after what happened felt like someone sitting on my chest. And nobody—nobody—asked if I was okay. Not even you."

That's what I'd want to say. But what would I actually say?
"I'm okay"?
That's not true.

But I'm not dead either.
That has to count for something.

I paused. Pressed the pen to my lip. There was a scuff mark on the ceiling above me that looked like a bird or a flame—depending on how you squinted.

I thought about my little sister. She's the only one I told. Just looked her in the eye and said, "I can't stay here."
She cried.
I didn't.

I hope she's okay. I hope she doesn't think I left *her*. She was the only reason I didn't burn that whole place down on my way out.

It took me walking, riding, begging, and hiding to make it to Covenant House. The Greyhound. The no's from people I called friends. Sleeping upright. Then the pay phone. The 9-line from the commercial.

Covenant didn't save me. But they fed me. Asked me if I was on drugs. Asked why I was there. I told them just enough. They gave me a sandwich and a spot on the girl side.

Some of those girls got dropped off like stray dogs. Because they were gay. Or pregnant. Or just too mouthy. But me?

I came because nobody was coming for me. Because something got taken from me, and nobody wanted to look that ugly truth in the face.

Now I'm here.

Rights of Passage. New rules. New key. New bunk. I don't know if I like it yet.

But I'm still here.
And that still counts.

I closed the notebook and tucked it under my pillow. I wasn't ready to tell anybody those things out loud. Not yet. But the page didn't judge me.

The page let me be complicated.
Let me tell the truth in my own time.
Let me bleed without cleaning it up first.

Outside, I could hear a girl laughing down the hall. Someone slammed a door. The building was coming alive again.

It was almost time to meet whoever slept on the bottom bunk.

And time to find out what "chores" really meant around here.

But for now, I just laid there.

Breathing.

Because this time, I could.

CHAPTER 3

Shelters & Shadows

"The world breaks everyone, and afterward, some are strong at the broken places."
— Ernest Hemingway

"Landslide"
– Fleetwood Mac

I was still lying on the top bunk when the door creaked open.

She came in like someone who'd done this a dozen times. Keys jingling, bag slung over one shoulder, hair pulled back in a neat bun that said she didn't have time for foolishness. She didn't even look up at me right away— just walked straight to the small closet, kicked off her shoes, and exhaled like her bones had been waiting all day for that sound.

"Hey," she said, finally glancing up. "You must be the new one."

I sat up, still unsure of the rules. "Yeah. Ruth."

She nodded like she already knew that. "I'm Tasha. I work mornings. Always get back around this time. Group's at six. You'll want to come."

That was it. No interrogation. No prying. Just a name and a routine.

She moved with a kind of practiced rhythm. Changed into sweats, peeled a protein bar from her bag, and settled into the chair by the window with a book. Not a word wasted. Not a step unsure.

It calmed me, honestly.

Like...okay. Maybe things don't have to spin all the time. Maybe a day can have edges. A shape.

I found myself counting the minutes until six, just because Tasha had mentioned it so calmly.

The group room was bigger than I expected, with folding chairs set up in a loose circle. No desks. No podium. Just a circle. Like everybody was supposed to be equal in here.

Some girls already had their favorite spots—legs tucked up, arms crossed, eyes down. A few whispered to each other. One girl looked like she was ready to fight whoever so much as breathed wrong. I didn't blame her.

Tasha slid into her seat like clockwork. Same chair, I could tell. She gave me a small nod, the kind that said: *It's okay. Just sit.*

So I did.

The facilitator was a woman named Miss Bri. Younger than I expected. Her hair was natural, twisted into chunky coils, and she wore Converse with her business slacks. She looked like somebody's big cousin—not too old, not too soft, but not trying to impress anybody either.

"Alright, ladies," she said, clapping her hands once. "We're here. New day. Clean slate."

Everyone quieted. Even the fighter.

"We've got a new face," Miss Bri added, glancing at me. "Wanna introduce yourself, or should I throw you a lifeline?"

I blinked. Cleared my throat.

"I'm Ruth," I said. "Just got here."

A few nods. One half-smile. Mostly unreadable reactions. That was fine. I didn't need applause. I just needed to be seen without being stared at.

"Well, Ruth," Miss Bri said warmly, "welcome. We're not perfect, but we try hard. And we start every group with a check-in. You'll get the hang of it."

One by one, the girls spoke.

"I'm good today. Got a call from my sister." "I'm tired, but I didn't cuss out nobody, so that's a win." "I'm anxious. I got an interview tomorrow."

Nothing too deep. But not fake, either. Honest in their own way.

When it came back around to me, I shrugged. "Still figuring things out."

That got a few quiet mhmm's. Not pity. Just... recognition.

I could get used to that.

Later that night, Tasha hung a hoodie on the back of the

chair and climbed into bed without saying much. I stayed awake longer, listening to her soft breathing, the hum of a streetlamp outside the window, the creak of the old building settling into night.

For the first time in weeks, I didn't feel like I had to watch my back. Not because I was safe, necessarily. But because I wasn't the only one trying to be.

And maybe—just maybe—tomorrow would have edges too.

The house had rules. Structure. Schedules. It wasn't prison, but it wasn't freedom either. Still, after sleeping in Greyhound stations and strange apartments, it was something steady—something warm. I took it.

Chores rotated every week. I got lucky that first round—dishes and dining room sweep. Some of the girls grumbled about scrubbing toilets, but not me. Not when I'd just clawed my way out of cold bus benches and borrowed showers. A mop and a broom? Please. That felt like luxury.

Then came the job hunt.

"You've got six months," the caseworker told me, clipboard in hand. Her voice wasn't unkind, just firm.

"After that, we transition you out. You get a job, you save money—we even hold part of your paycheck to help with a deposit when you leave."

That sounded good. In theory.

But bus routes in a city that didn't care about poor Black girls? That was a different thing. My friend Cola had my back, though. She was my ace. Always looking out. She slipped me extra tokens like they were gold coins.

"Don't waste them," she whispered one night, sliding two into my hand like a secret. "Hit the strip early. Ask everywhere. Hostess jobs, diners, even the warehouse store. Act like it's already yours."

She was a hostess at some Mexican place, and one day she dragged me along. Told the staff it was my birthday just for fun. Next thing I knew, there was singing and clapping and cake in my face. I pretended to be mad. But honestly? I hadn't smiled like that in months. I still owe her for that. Haven't seen her since.

Then there was Chris. Or Christine. Or Christopher. S/he was transitioning—cool, chill, quiet. People stared sometimes, but Chris held their head up anyway. I respected that. I didn't say much—I still wasn't used to the way girls in that place acted like privacy wasn't a thing. Walked in on you in the bathroom like it was normal.

"We all got the same thing," they'd say.

"That don't mean shit," I'd mutter.

By month four, I had no job. I had interviewed at seven different places. Nothing stuck. Either I didn't have the right clothes, or I didn't look the part. I started tagging along with the girls who had shifts—watching how they clocked in, smiled for tips, played the part. Maybe I could play the part too.

When the time came to leave Rights of Passage, it wasn't some triumphant moment. There was no "You Go Girl" award, no balloon send-off. Just a small folder, a schedule of bus routes, and a caseworker saying, "You've done what you could here. It's time."

Some of the girls looked at me like I was lucky. A few of the older ones—jaded, bitter—just rolled their eyes.

"Don't get too excited," one said. "Out there's worse than in here."

Maybe she was right. Maybe she wasn't. I just knew I had to keep moving.

It started with couch surfing. A friend of a friend. Then

———••●❋●••———

that friend's boyfriend started staring too long. That stare—too hungry, too lingering—had a weight that told me it was time to go.

The second apartment came from a number in my memory. A woman I knew from my last stretch in Houston. She answered, surprised but warm. "You still in town?" she asked. I lied and said I was just passing through. She invited me to a church event—some kind of revival service. I didn't care what it was. I was just grateful for a place to go where the air didn't smell like stale beer and old secrets.

But church people got eyes. And they used them. Judged with their glances, whispered behind their hymnals. I could hear it in the tight way they said, *God bless you*, like it was an apology. Or a warning. The woman pulled strings and found me a shelter—or at least, that's what she called it.

It was more like a place death forgot. An old, half-burned motel out near the tracks. The kind of place you see in a movie right before someone screams. My "room" was a cracked mattress on the floor surrounded by peeling walls and sounds that didn't belong to the living. I laid on top of the sheets, arms folded, praying nothing bit me. Across the hall, I swear the door opened by itself. I didn't sleep. Just stared at the ceiling and counted the water stains like stars.

One night. That's all I gave it.

The third place should've been better. Should've. Another girl from my past said I could crash with her. I barely had time to sit down before she started accusing me of eyeing her man. He hadn't even looked in my direction. Or maybe he had. Either way, I was too tired to fight about it. I left before she could finish her sentence.

I was walking again.

At first, it was just to get air. Then I realized I had no destination. Nowhere to go. My feet took me to a laundromat. I laid down on the hard bench between washers, pretending I'd lost a bet. Told the couple who walked in that the winners were on the way to check on me. They laughed awkwardly. I smiled back like I wasn't cold and scared and two degrees from breaking.

Another night, I crashed in a parking garage—the far end, where nobody parks because it's dark and creepy. I tried to sleep, but a fat green caterpillar kept crawling toward my face. I shifted once, twice, three times. The damn thing followed me like it was on a mission. I whispered to it, "What you want from me?" like it could answer. Eventually, I gave up and found a stairwell. Curled into a corner.

People walked past like I wasn't even there.

That stung more than the cold.

There was no *Are you okay?* No *Do you need help?* Just indifference. Like I was a misplaced garbage bag someone meant to throw away. I wanted to scream, *Do you see me? I'm still a person.* But I stayed silent. Invisibility had its perks. No one can hurt you if they don't see you.
That was three months in.

Still homeless. Still moving.

I had a few bus tokens left. A couple quarters for a payphone. I'd stand across the street, pretending to read the numbers on the wall so old men wouldn't stare too long. But they always did. I could feel their eyes crawling across my skin like that damn caterpillar. One of them licked his lips. I nearly vomited.

Eventually, a boy named Brian offered me a ride. He had a brown station wagon and one of those confident smiles. I wasn't in the mood. My tone was sharp—*don't try me* sharp. He looked hurt and said, "Damn... what man hurt you?" I didn't answer. We both knew the question didn't need one.
He dropped me off at a Hispanic-only shelter. The woman who ran it spoke in broken English, told me the rules. All

I caught was, "Be here by five… or no come in." Curfew. Got it.

I stayed two nights. Barely left my room. The neighborhood was foreign. So were the faces. A man across the way tried to talk to me, but I didn't understand a word he said. I just kept nodding and backing away.

On the third day, I was downtown. Far. Too far.

I looked up and realized I had two hours to get back before curfew. I started running. Caught a bus. Then came the damn parade. Streets blocked. Beads flying. Music pounding like a heartbeat out of rhythm. People yelling, laughing, drunk on celebration. I tried to push through, but the crowd swallowed me whole.

By the time I made it back, I already knew I was out. The shelter lady barely looked at me. She handed me my red duffel and pointed toward the street. The man who'd been hitting on me waved goodbye. I waved back, still clueless about what he ever said to me.

So I walked.

No plan. No place.
Darkness crept in. I spotted a corner store in the distance, headed toward the glow of the streetlight. I sat under it for an hour, watching shadows stretch across pavement.

That's when the cop pulled up.

He asked why I was there.

"It's dark as hell," I said. "I ain't walking nowhere 'til the sun's up."

He stared at me like he didn't know what box to put me in. Then he opened the back door of his cruiser. "Come on."

My heart clenched. Was this it? Was this when the cuffs came?

But no. He drove me to a shelter.

It was for single moms and pregnant girls. I was neither, but they took me in anyway.

It was called Mercy House.

CHAPTER 4

Invisible In Plain Sight

"I've been broken. I've been humiliated. But I never stopped walking."
— Maya Angelou

"Oh, the Blood"
– New Jersey Mass Choir

Mercy House.

That's how they answered the phone. No matter the time of day. *"Mercy House. Good morning. Mercy House. Good evening. Mercy House."* Same voice. Same tone. Like they were daring the chaos to knock at the door and find peace already waiting.

It wasn't fancy, but it was clean. The lights buzzed overhead, and the paint on the walls was chipped in the corners—but it didn't smell like mold or regret. That was enough for me.

The laundry room was always booked. Thursdays if you were lucky. You had to sign your name on a little clipboard near the front. I'd sit by the window sometimes and just wait for my turn, watching traffic roll past like it had somewhere better to be. I never did.

There was a little boy who ran around like the place was his kingdom. Couldn't have been more than four, but he had big energy and no filter. He had this habit of naming people after food. Miss Tracy became "Pickle." Somebody else was "Lemon Pie." And me?

He called me *Peanut Butter.*

It stuck.

Every time he saw me, he'd yell it with his whole chest.

"PEANUT BUTTERRRRR!"

Like it was a badge. And maybe it was. Maybe being named something sweet meant I didn't look as bitter as I felt.

One day, a new girl came in. And I swear, I almost fell out.

It was a girl from Rights of Passage. I blinked three times, thought maybe I was hallucinating. But nope—it was her. We never said much to each other back then, but that day? Seeing a familiar face hit different. Like, *Okay. I'm not the only one still wandering.*

We nodded at each other like survivors in a war zone. No words needed. Just, *You still breathing? Me too. Cool.*

Now... don't judge me.

God's still working on me.

Somebody stole some pads. Not me—I mean, maybe me. Look, I'm not saying who took them. All I'm saying is, one day they came up missing. The lady who needed them started hollering, and the whole house got searched. One at a time. In the bathroom. Like we were smuggling contraband.

I don't know where *she* hid them. But *she* didn't get caught.
That same day, *she* walked to the corner store with fifty cents and a prayer. Told the manager she'd work two hours in exchange for a pack. He looked at her, took the change, and pointed to the door.

That pack didn't walk out of that store. But somehow, she did.

And *God protected her.*
Won't He do it.

Mercy House didn't last long after that.

We'd barely been there a month when the staff started acting different. Meetings behind closed doors. Extra inspections. One day, they told us to pack our things—they were shutting down for "safety and compliance updates." That's the phrase they used. But we all knew what it really meant: no funding. No help. No home.

I was devastated.

I'd finally started to sleep through the night again. I was starting to believe I might be okay. That maybe I could rebuild. But in an instant, it was over. Just like that.

Back to the streets. Back to uncertainty. Back to the ache of having *almost* found somewhere safe.

I cried in the stairwell that night. Didn't even try to hide it.

One of the staff members offered me a granola bar and a ride to a nearby park. I didn't want either.

I wanted a second chance.

But life wasn't handing those out.

So I went back to what I knew. Back to Street Wise.

It was a day shelter—cool inside, quiet, safe. You had to be unhoused to even get in. They checked.

They had food—cup noodles, stale donuts, gas station pizza, and that lukewarm coffee that tasted like yesterday. But it was something. And it was free.

Some days, that was enough to feel like hope.

They had showers too. You had to sign up early, though. First come, first clean. I'd write my name slow and deliberate, watching the line grow behind me. Some folks scribbled Xs. Some just made up letters. They didn't care. Street Wise just needed headcounts for the grant money.

One day, I filled out paperwork. All of it.

They said, *"If you stick with the program, we can help you get an apartment. But there's a wait. Six months."*

Six months?

I wanted to laugh. *Six months? Girl, I don't know where*

I'm sleeping tonight.

I went back to Covenant House. Not officially, just... wandered there like it still owed me something. One of the staff remembered me. She let me sleep in the church for the night. Said I had to be out by six. No problem. Six a.m. is mercy compared to sleeping in stairwells with strangers stepping over you like trash.

I found this little book someone gave me—a directory of shelters, food banks, churches that passed out sandwiches and lukewarm juice boxes. When I had $2, I'd buy a day pass for the bus.

Pro tip: Buy it at 10 p.m. That way, it lasts until the next night.

Stretch that 24 hours like it's currency.

One night, I went back to a place I used to hang around— just seeing if anyone I knew was still around. I started talking to a security guard. He had a nice smile, and I was tired of pretending to be invisible.

Next thing I know, I'm living with him. Sort of.

He told his wife I was his cousin.

I found out I was his "cousin" the same day his mama came to visit. She looked at me sideways and said, *"Who's this?"*

His wife said, *"That's your niece."*

His mama said, *"No it ain't."*
The silence after that?

Whew.

We just stood there like someone hit pause on the whole room. Mouths open. Eyes darting. Me sweating.

But guess what?

They let me stay.

His wife had just had a baby, so maybe she was too tired to fight. Or maybe they figured, *What's done is done.* Either way, I stayed. Helped out. Bought groceries with my EBT. I'd go to the store with him, hand over the food stamp card, and come back with bread and milk and those little frozen burritos that burn your mouth if you're not careful.

We were one big... slightly dysfunctional... almost happy... family. Family-ish.

His wife always thought I wanted him.

Puh-lease.

I was just grateful for the roof, the warmth, and not waking up under a flickering streetlight again.

I'd been at the security guard's house for a few weeks when I pulled out my notebook again. The green one with the bent corner. The one that's been riding with me since the first shelter. It smelled like old paper and corner stores, and it always found its way back to my hands when I needed to hear myself.

I sat on the back step after everyone had gone to bed. The baby had finally stopped crying. The neighborhood was quiet except for the occasional dog barking like it was chasing ghosts. I didn't have much to write with—just a chewed-up pen and the voice in my head.

I don't even know what day it is.

I've been living as someone's cousin. I've been sleeping on borrowed time, under borrowed roofs. I've had full days where no one asked my name.

But I'm still here.

Some nights I miss my little sister so bad my chest hurts. I wonder what she's doing—if she still talks about me in the present tense. If my mama is mad, or worried, or if she's just trying to keep the family from asking too many questions.

I haven't called. Still don't know what I'd say. *"Hey, Ma. I left. I couldn't breathe. I should've said more, but I didn't know how to explain the way my world cracked open after what happened. I didn't want to carry it. I didn't want to carry them."*

Maybe that's what hurts the most—how fast I thought people expected me to move on. Pretend like it didn't happen. Like my body wasn't marked. Like my silence was agreement.

But it wasn't.

I'm proud of myself. Even if I still don't know what I'm doing. Even if all I've got is this pen and this page. I'm proud because I didn't lay down and die. I kept waking up. I kept going to Street Wise. I kept figuring out where the next meal might come from. I never stopped looking for light.

And maybe that's what surviving looks like.

Surviving doesn't mean you're never afraid. It means you don't let fear make your decisions for you. It means you keep walking—even if you've got nothing but pain in your pockets.

Some days, I feel like I've been loved—but only a little. Loved in pieces. In pity. In almosts. Not chosen. Not held. Not fully seen.

But that's okay.

Because I see me.
And I'm not ashamed of the girl who walked out of that house with five dollars and a can of corn.

I don't regret leaving. But I do wish I had known I didn't have to carry all of it. I took on the full weight of what he did—like it was mine to carry. Like surviving meant proving something. But surviving means releasing too.

So this is me, learning to let go. Of the guilt. Of the shame. Of the lie that says I was supposed to be stronger. I was strong enough to leave. Strong enough to stay alive. Strong enough to keep healing, even when it's ugly and lonely and slow.

If you're reading this, and you're somewhere out there trying to find your next step: Keep going.

You're not broken beyond repair. You're not too late. You're not too far gone.

You're here. That means something.

I put the notebook down on my lap and wiped my face with the sleeve of a too-big hoodie. It smelled like fabric softener and old survival.

Tomorrow, I'd go look for work again. Someone had mentioned a movie theater near the bus stop.

Maybe they'd hire me.

And if they didn't?

I'd keep walking.

Because that's what I do.

CHAPTER 5

Popcorn & Petty

"Life is tough, my darling, but so are you."
— Stephanie Bennett-Henry

"You Brought the Sunshine"
— The Clark Sisters

There was something holy about the smell of popcorn at 9 a.m.

It clung to your skin, slid under your fingernails, soaked into your clothes until it became a second scent. Sweet, greasy, and oddly comforting. The Regal 18 wasn't glamorous. It was old. The seats creaked, the tiles in the lobby were cracked, and the carpet had a weird maroon-and-navy galaxy swirl pattern that had definitely seen better days. But to me? It was sanctuary. A place with a clock-in time and a breakroom fridge. A place where nobody cared if you were rebuilding yourself from rubble.

The theater had its own rhythm. The lobby filled slowly in the mornings with the sound of shoe soles sticking to floors that had been mopped with soda instead of water. The men's restroom near Theater 3 had a toilet that overflowed weekly. If you were unlucky enough to be on shift that day, the stench greeted you halfway down the hallway. It was theater life—loud, messy, weirdly consistent.

I was staying with the security guard and his family when I landed the job. My first real job. It gave me a reason to wake up and try. I started off in concessions, and that's when I learned something important: concession work is not for the faint of heart. Especially when you're left-handed and living in a right-handed world.

The scoop? A nightmare. The cash register? Might as well have been a spaceship.

They trained us fast, barking instructions over the whir of soda machines and the endless loop of trailers playing in the background. I tried. I did. But I was slow, awkward. Burned my arm once reaching for hot nacho cheese and nearly cried when I dropped an entire tray of popcorn mid-rush.

Every Thursday we had a team meeting in the lobby. And every Thursday, I was the unspoken main event. People didn't say my name, but their eyes did. Their tone did.

"We need to talk about accuracy." "We need to talk about speed."

Eventually, I stood up, hands on my hips, and said, "We all
know this is about me. So let's stop pretending. Whoever wants to switch positions, let's do it. You don't like me. I don't like y'all. Let's make peace."

That's how I ended up at the door. And baby, I *owned* that door.

The Bomb Scare

One of the standees—those giant cardboard movie cutouts—had these cool blinking lights. I asked management if I could take the lights when they tossed the standee. They said yes. So I did. I packed them into my red duffel and forgot all about it.

A few days later, laundry day ran long. I brought my bag straight to work and tucked it behind another display in the lobby. It was a quiet morning. I did my rounds, chatted with coworkers, and didn't think twice about the duffel.

When I went to grab something from it... gone.

"Y'all seen my laundry?" I asked, walking into the breakroom.

I found my bag sitting on a chair near the manager's office. Their faces? Suspicious. Pale. Like they'd seen a ghost. Turns out they were *this close* to calling the cops. Said they saw wires poking out and thought it was a bomb.

"A *bomb*?!" I said. "Those are from the standee! Y'all told me I could have them."

They admitted the only reason they hesitated was because they saw my name on a keychain attached to the zipper.

"Next time," one manager said, still shaken, "maybe just... let someone know when you're bringing something weird."

I rolled my eyes. "Y'all want a full inventory of my laundry detergent while I'm at it?"

We all laughed. Sort of.

The Petty Part

Then there was Rick.

Rick was a manager with a clipboard and a God complex. One morning, someone in box office no-showed. I offered to help. He waved me off with, "You'll never get it."

Okay.

Half an hour later, guess who came crawling back?

"Can you help me out now?" he asked.

I smiled, crossed my legs, and said, "Nah. I probably wouldn't get it."

Petty? Yep.

Delicious? Oh, absolutely.

Rick & America's Most Wanted

Karma doesn't sleep.

One afternoon, I'm working door when an entire SWAT van rolls up outside. Full tactical gear. Bulletproof everything. My stomach dropped.

They got me. It's about the toilet paper I took. (Don't judge me.)

Turns out, they weren't there for me. They were there for Rick.

Well, they thought they were.
Rick had a doppelganger—a *perfect* match to someone featured on *America's Most Wanted.* When the episode aired, folks called the theater non-stop. His face was that close to the guy on the list.

It wasn't him. But the buzz? Hilarious.

I grinned, "That's what you get for not letting me work the box."

The Bushes

Then one day, we got a heads-up: VIP guests coming. Act right. Don't breathe funny.

When the motorcade pulled up—a line of black SUVs,

polished to a shine so bright you could see your reflection—I thought, *Either it's Jesus, or we're about to host a press conference.*

Nope.

It was George and Barbara Bush.

They were smaller in person. Fragile-looking almost. Barbara wore a pale pink blouse, neatly pressed slacks, and pearls. George had on khakis and a navy windbreaker. Both of them smelled faintly like old cologne, sunscreen, and money.

Their security detail was massive. A blur of black suits, radios, and mirrored sunglasses. The air shifted when they walked in. Everyone stood up straighter. I scanned their tickets like I was being tested by the Secret Service.

"Theater 7," I said, my voice steady, but my hands not so much.

George nodded. Barbara smiled.

They didn't speak much. But their presence? Heavy. Like the moment had been ironed into history.

The Theater After Dark

Here's the thing about working in a movie theater: once the sun goes down, it turns into a different world.

We had couples who thought the dark was an invitation for things that should've stayed private. One pair got caught in Theater 12 doing something that almost got them arrested. They tried to play it off like they were looking for a lost phone. I guess they thought the floor was a good place to search... in that position.

Then there were the families sneaking in food like it was a mission from God. Whole rotisserie chickens. Crockpots. One woman had a baby stroller that didn't even have a baby in it—just three bags of takeout from Luby's.

Kids would sneak in through the side exit by Theater 6. You could always tell. They'd smell like outside. Not sweat—*outside*. That combination of Axe body spray and mischief.

And then there was the man we nicknamed "Double Feature Dan."

He'd buy one ticket and stay all day. Move from theater to theater with the precision of a Navy SEAL. He had a rotation. Knew the showtimes better than the managers.

Nobody ever caught him red-handed, but we all knew. We just let him live. That man had seen *Finding Nemo* fourteen times. In a row.

The job didn't save me. But it gave me a place to be. To be *seen.*

The theater was messy, loud, frustrating. But it was mine.

And in the middle of surviving, it gave me popcorn butter under my nails, George Bush's smile, a petty win against Rick, and just enough light to keep going.

One Last Twist of Good

Somewhere in all that, the theater payphone started ringing. Like… every morning.

I'd be walking up the steps, and it would start ringing like it was waiting for me. I answered it three times—nothing. Just silence on the other end. So I stopped picking up. Just grabbed it, hung it up, kept walking. It went on for about six months.

Then it stopped.

No explanation.

No closure.

Just like a lot of things in my life back then. But still—good times were had by all. Except Rick. That's what he gets.

Back home, I was still staying with the couple. Still trying to save. Still trying to get out. I'd been in line for my own apartment for months, praying, waiting, hoping. Then one day, I got the call.

A girl ahead of me in line got into a fight and was kicked out of the program.

And just like that—*my* name moved up.

I was getting an apartment.

I hung up the phone and whispered, "Thank you, Jesus," like He'd been waiting on me to say it.

All the people who had done me wrong, all the ones who thought I wouldn't make it, all the little indignities I swallowed with a smile... none of it mattered in that moment. I was about to have my own keys. My own space.

I was about to have a door that locked from the inside.

CHAPTER 6

The Bridge and the Break

*"I survived because the fire inside me burned brighter
than the fire around me."*
—Joshua Graham

"Yesterday"
- Mary Mary

"I see there's an incident listed on your behavioral health summary from last year," the intake counselor said, flipping her file open with a soft click of the tab.

She didn't say it with judgment. Just procedure. It was a checklist item—like allergies, emergency contact, and whether or not I had cookware.

"Yeah," I said. "That was a thing."

She nodded. "No problem—it's not a barrier. I just need to document it. Add your statement and attach a safety notation to your file. For our records and yours. This is a supported housing program, so we stay ahead of anything that could raise concerns down the line."

Her tone was gentle, professional. But it still made me shift in my chair.

She kept writing. "Take your time. Just walk me through what happened."

I shrugged. "It wasn't anything wild. I didn't need a padded room or a therapist or anything. I had a moment. You want the real story?"

She smiled, pen still in hand. "Always."

This was early theater days. I was still living with the couple—the security guard and his wife. They were good to me. Gave me space. Encouragement. I was getting steady hours, my uniform didn't smell like anxiety anymore, and for once, I didn't feel like I was running.

So one day, feeling extra hopeful, I decided I wanted to go back to school.

They had a real phone—landline, spiral cord, mounted on the wall of the third-floor hallway. I climbed the stairs like I was climbing toward something real, something mine.

I called Student Services.

The lady was polite. Sweet, even. But the second she pulled up my file, her voice changed.

"You still owe a balance," she said. "We can't proceed with your re-enrollment until that's cleared."

I said what I always said when life pushed back. "Well, I guess I'll go jump off a bridge, then. That should make your day easier."

And I hung up.

Didn't think twice. I had a stank attitude and a sharp tongue. No filter. No real sense of consequence.

Within five minutes, the police were at the door.

"Ma'am, are you Ruth?"

"Yes."

"We need you to come with us."

They didn't cuff me. Not at first. I wasn't resisting. Just

confused and low-key amused. Like, *Y'all serious?*
Then Lauryn Hill came on the radio—*Killing Me Softly*—
and I cracked up. The absurdity of it all hit me sideways.
I remember leaning against the cold window in the
backseat of that patrol car thinking, *Well, this is definitely
not how I thought today would go.*

They took me to the psych emergency room. I was
handcuffed to a bolted-down chair for twelve hours, in a
waiting room that smelled like floor cleaner and
hopelessness.

Real patients were in there. Folks talking to themselves.
People pacing. One woman was arguing with a wall-
mounted soap dispenser like it had ruined her marriage. I
just sat there, my bad attitude crumpled in my lap like a
dirty napkin.

Eventually, I was called back to see a nurse. She looked
me up and down and started her script:

"How are you feeling? Do you have a plan to hurt
yourself? Are you hearing voices?"

I told her what happened. Gave it to her straight.

She blinked once and said, "Okay. Here's what you do:
stop telling people *you're* gonna jump off a bridge. Tell
them to go jump off a bridge."

Then she closed her folder and said, "You're not mentally ill. You just have an attitude."

Back in the intake office, the counselor chuckled softly. "Thank you for sharing that. I'll make a note that it was a one-time statement, no current ideation, resolved. That's what we call it in the system: resolved."

I nodded, watching her write.

"Ruth," she added, meeting my eyes, "this is just something we document to protect you. Not label you."

That meant more than she knew.

Outside, the couple's little gray car was still running, packed to the roof with everything I owned—Goodwill finds, a box TV, a set of hand-me-down dishes, and a tangle of thrift store hope. The apartment was mine now. Keys in my hand. A door that locked from the inside.

So yeah, I had an incident on file.

But I also had a future.

There are some moments that don't hit you until later. Quiet betrayals that whisper instead of scream. Moments where someone crosses a line you didn't even know needed guarding—until it's too late.

The Husband

It happened not long after I moved into the apartment. The couple who'd taken me in—the security guard and his wife—had helped pack my things, loaded their little gray car with all my Goodwill treasures, and drove me across town like I was family.

I thought they were safe.

So I didn't know what to do when he asked me, halfway up the stairs, *"When can I get a copy of your key?"*

I paused. Confused.

"For what?"

"To check on you," he said. Smiled like it was normal. Like it made sense.

I looked him dead in the eye and said, "You can call."

Just like that.

I haven't seen them since.

Part of me wondered if I overreacted. But another part—stronger, louder—knew I hadn't. The wife had *just* had a baby. He had never said anything out of line before. Never looked at me sideways. But that question? That moment? It told me everything I needed to know.

He thought I owed him something for helping me survive. He thought access was a fair trade for kindness.

But I knew better.

I may not have had much in my life at the time, but what I did have—my body, my boundaries, my key—belonged to me.

I didn't tattle. Didn't drag his name through the mud. But I left that situation exactly where it needed to stay: behind me. I wasn't gonna be the kind of woman who gave warnings to other women while burning in silence. I just removed myself.

That ain't me, Corbin. That ain't me.

Jai'Da

Life had evened out for a minute. I was working steady hours at the theater, actually enjoying it again. Eating popcorn without crying, laughing with customers, living light. Then Jai'Da came.

She was new. Quiet. Soft-spoken, which made her easy to work with. I was still on the door; she was in concessions. We weren't friends at first, but we started talking. She gave me a ride home one day, and that was it—we started hanging out here and there. It felt nice to have someone to laugh with.

Until she ruined it.

I had a guy who made rings. Beautiful silver ones. I love rings—always have. They made me feel dressed, even when I had nothing but thrifted jeans and a hoodie. I'd saved up and was getting a new one made. Jai'Da offered to drive me to pick it up.

His name was Neal. We weren't dating. We'd never even hugged. He just made my rings, and I paid in cash or in hours worked at the theater. That was it.

So we're sitting there, waiting for Neal to come back with

my order, and she says—out of nowhere—"I'll take him from you."

I blinked. Thought maybe I misheard her.
But no. She leaned in again and said it louder. "I'll take him from you."

I didn't even flinch. I just nodded, said, "Cool," and sat quiet the rest of the ride home. But in my head? I was DONE.

It wasn't what she said. It was the *fact* that she said it.

What if he *had* been my man? What kind of woman says something like that and thinks it's cute?

There was no misunderstanding. That was a *choice* she made—to slice at me, sideways and smiling. I never spoke to her again. The next day at work, I didn't look her way. Didn't breathe her direction.

Everyone kept asking what was wrong. I just said, "Ask Jai'Da."

I left it there.

In hindsight, I realize those moments mattered more than

I knew. I wasn't just walking away from drama—I was walking toward *self-worth.* I was learning, slowly, that protecting your peace doesn't require permission. That setting boundaries isn't about being rude, it's about being *alive.*

Ruth was growing—even when I didn't know I was.

Even when the world tried to tell me I was too broken to draw lines.

Even when kindness came with strings.
I didn't snap. I didn't stoop. I didn't need to throw punches or yell.

I just... stepped back into myself.

And kept walking.

There's something about living on your own for the first time that feels like flight. Even if your wings are made of trauma and duct tape, you're still soaring—until the wind shifts.

I was twenty-two with my own apartment, a job I didn't hate, and a Walkman that stayed on full blast. Nobody could tell me nothing. And that was the problem.

Freedom felt like running barefoot through traffic. I was

determined to touch every part of life I missed while surviving. Friends, crushes, missteps—I wanted it all. But there's a line between curiosity and chaos, and back then I couldn't always see it.

We had theater passes that let us go see movies at other locations. Every spot had a different vibe. One place had this older lady—Buela energy all the way. You could tell she came from some ancient wisdom, like her spirit had been seasoned for generations. I'd sit with her in the lobby, forget the movie I came for, and just listen. Never found out if she was Native or Hispanic, but she had that rooted soul you don't question. Just sit and receive.

Another theater had a guy behind concessions who liked me a little too much. Every time I came in, he'd slide me a candy bag full of stale nachos—cheese cup hidden at the bottom like a secret. You weren't technically allowed to get cheese unless you paid. But he always hooked me up.

"Don't say I never gave you anything," he'd wink.

It was harmless. Funny. A little weird. But at the time, that kind of attention filled a part of me that still felt invisible. I didn't see it as dangerous. I saw it as kindness. Now, I know better. There's a difference.

The theater itself was its own soap opera. Donnie and Kyle were best friends—one rich, one barely scraping by. But they stuck together like brothers. They'd give me rides, buy me snacks, argue about movies. One smoked on every break. Another tried to flirt by writing me up at work.

"You just lost your chance," I told him, tearing the write-up slip in half like a love letter.

I didn't finish cleaning the concession counter that night.

The bus was coming. I had to roll out.

And I did.

I was such a thug. One day I jumped off the bus instead of stepping down like a normal person. Sprained my ankle. Ended up in the ER. The nurse who assisted me had been a passenger on the same bus that day.

"The way you jumped out, I *knew* it'd be you," the nurse said, wrapping my foot with a shake of her head.

She wasn't wrong.

I didn't drink. Never smoked. Not then, not now. But one night, I was thirsty. Like, desert-thirsty. No matter how much water or juice I drank, I still felt dry. So when Neal—the ring guy—came over with his Bud Ice Lite, I made a decision.

"I'm relieving you of all responsibilities," I told him, reaching for the can. "Let me just have one."

He said no.

I drank it anyway.

Then another. Then another. Then three more.

Still thirsty.
The room spun so hard, I thought I was on a ride at the State Fair. My toilet and I got spiritually married that night. And Neal—he just shook his head.

"Told you," he said.

He still helped me. Rubbed my back. Got me water and a blanket.

That was the night I learned a valuable lesson. That kind of thirst wasn't physical. It was soul-deep. And beer wasn't the answer.

Looking back, I know now what I didn't know then: I was mentally unwell.

Not "crazy," not "too far gone," not broken.

Just... burdened.

Trauma that goes unspoken doesn't disappear. It mutates. It shows up in weird behavior, risky decisions, laughter that covers screams. I had survived a sexual assault and never unpacked it. Never sat with it. Never named it out loud.

Instead, I stayed busy.

Worked.
Laughed.
Played.
Experimented.
Ignored the storm forming in the background.

That's how mental health struggles work sometimes. You don't see the breakdown coming. You just notice one day that you're not okay. You wake up and the weight in your chest won't move. You go to a movie and can't focus. You listen to music but feel nothing. You start skipping meals. Or skipping feelings. Or skipping people.

The National Institute of Mental Health calls it "persistent depressive disorder." Low-level sadness that lingers like a dull ache in your bones. Paired with trauma? It's gasoline on an already slow-burning fire.

And I didn't have a therapist. I had coworkers, buses, nachos, and music.

I was trying. But trying isn't the same as healing.

It all came crashing down with a trip to the rental office.

I went in to pay rent—on time, proud—and the lady behind the desk looked at me like I was trash on her porch.
"When your lease is up, don't bother renewing," she said.

"What?"

"We've had multiple complaints. Your music is too loud."

I blinked. Reached into my bag and pulled out my Walkman. "This? Lady, if I'm disturbing people with this, I'd be deaf."

She didn't care. Didn't want to listen. I don't even think it was about the music.

So about a month later, I moved out. Packed up my little life and went back home. No fireworks. No goodbye party. Just... gone.

And that's when I realized: I had done everything right—kept to myself, paid my rent, followed the rules—and still got tossed.

Sometimes life will evict you, even when you color inside the lines.

I'm not telling you this for pity.
I'm telling you because it's true.

Because some of us grow up thinking if we just do enough, smile enough, survive enough—we'll finally be safe. But safety isn't found in apartments or friendships or jobs. It's found in truth.

My truth is that I was young. I made mistakes. I had wounds I didn't know how to heal.

But I never stopped trying to live. I never stopped walking toward the version of me that refused to be ruined.

CHAPTER 7

The Flowers at the Door

"The darkest nights produce the brightest stars."
—John Green

"When You've Been Blessed"
– Patti LaBelle

It was around '99 when I moved back to Houston. I was older now, but still raw. Still running from some parts of myself I didn't want to face. Didn't have a job, barely had food, but I had my own apartment—and that meant something.

Bills got paid through God, grit, and whatever charity could help me scrape by. Temp jobs came and went. I kept a referral book like it was a Bible—dog-eared, coffee-stained, full of circles and arrows and hope. I hit up every place I could, whether they gave out hot meals or day-old donuts. Some days all I got was a sandwich and a prayer. Still, it was something.

One morning I woke up hungry and determined. Called a number in the book, and they told me where to go. It was one of those early-riser setups—like, *you gotta get up with Jesus* type early.

I got there late.

The line was already wrapped around the block like it was Black Friday. The people, we were a mix of stories and sorrows.

In front of me stood a white woman in her fifties wearing a faded pink bathrobe and men's sneakers, no laces. Her hair was matted in the back, like she'd slept sitting up. Beside her, a tall Black man with a long gray beard and one arm in a sling. He wore worn-down boots and a military jacket two sizes too big. Said nothing. Just stared ahead like he'd been in this line a hundred times before.

Behind me, there was a short Asian man with wire-framed glasses and a blue windbreaker. He held a reusable grocery tote that had holes in it, and he kept humming something under his breath. Gospel maybe? I didn't ask. Then there was a Hispanic lady with three kids, all under seven. The youngest sat in a stroller with no front wheel. Her oldest held onto her waist like he was

afraid she might disappear.
We all looked different.

But we were there for the same reason.

Two dogs barked nearby—one tied to a street sign with a shoelace, the other curled up under a blanket next to a sleeping man with a cardboard sign that read: "Still trying."

I stood there confused, empty-handed, until this kind-faced man—let's call him Jose—noticed I didn't have any grocery bags.

He didn't ask questions. He just handed me his extras and smiled like he'd known me all my life. Didn't speak much English, but kindness don't need translation.

Turns out the line was for a house, not a store. A single-story home converted into a pantry. The inside smelled like boiled rice, cheap hand sanitizer, and old shoes. The kind of scent that clings to your coat after you've been there too long. The floors creaked, and fans buzzed from every corner trying to keep the heat at bay. You could hear the low murmur of folks thanking people under their breath, plastic bags rustling, kids fussing quietly.

Volunteers were everywhere. A Black woman with tight twists, blue eyeliner, and a clip-on name badge motioned us forward. She wore a T-shirt that read "Bless Somebody Today." At the scoop station, a white man in his sixties cracked jokes while holding a scoop the size of a cereal bowl. He had food stains on his jeans and the kind of face that looked like it had seen too much and kept going anyway.

And then there was the older Asian man in the corner, slicing day-old bread into smaller portions and gently handing them to the children first. I caught his eye. He nodded.

We moved in groups. Quietly. Carefully. Three scoops per bin—rice, beans, pasta, oatmeal. I filled my bags with red beans, lima beans, and white rice. Scooped each one like I was borrowing grace. At the end of the house was a long table covered in baked goods: honey buns still in plastic, squashed apple pies in flimsy boxes, and a pile of Twinkies that looked like they'd been stacked and restacked since Tuesday.

I grabbed a mix. Sweet things felt like little victories.

Next came the hygiene table. I took what I could: one off-brand tube of toothpaste with a bent cap, a bar of Irish Spring soap wrapped in cracked green plastic, two rolls of toilet tissue so thin you could read through them, and a 30-pack of Q-tips in a torn cardboard sleeve. I slipped a pack of maxi pads into my coat pocket like they were gold. Because some days, they were.

There was a section for kids too—diapers, rattles, books with chewed corners—but I kept moving. That wasn't my season.

I walked out the back of the house with my bags heavy and my heart heavier. Circled around the front, found a bus stop three blocks away. Sat down and exhaled.

On the ride home, I clutched my bags like they might fly away. I didn't look at anyone. Just stared out the window and whispered a prayer.

"God, thank you for showing up in strange places. Thank you for Twinkies and red beans. Thank you for people who give without asking. Thank you for not letting me feel invisible today. Thank you for Jose, and the woman with the T-shirt, and the man with the bread, and even for the woman in the robe. Lord, help me hold onto this peace. I know it might not last, but let me remember how this feels the next time I'm back on empty. Let me remember that this struggle doesn't mean I'm forgotten. That I can still be seen. Still be helped. Still be held in Your care."

It was a quiet ride. But inside me, something stirred.

Still, rejection has a way of creeping back in.

One time, I went to a church pantry. They told me I couldn't come back for six months—I'd come too often. As if hunger had a schedule.

One charity refused to help with my $25 water bill because it was "too low." Said I could've found *someone* to cover it. Another mega church, big building, bold choir—told me flat out: no help unless I was a member.

I smiled and left.

But inside, I broke a little.

It felt like I was being punished for trying to survive with dignity. I was doing what I could, not begging, not stealing, just *asking.* But it was never enough. Never quite the right look, or the right reason, or the right moment.

One woman even told me, "You don't look like you belong here."

I wanted to ask her what struggling was supposed to look like. Dirty? Crying? Collapsed on the floor?

But I didn't say a word. Just took my pride, folded it into my purse, and walked out. Because that's what I did back then—collected my bruises in silence.

And yet... amid all that rejection, came small moments of grace.

Like the day someone left flowers at the front desk for me back when I worked at the movie theater. Just a regular day. I was walking past the box office and saw the prettiest bouquet sitting on the floor.

I leaned over and said, "Those are nice. You got a secret admirer or something?"

The girl in box smiled. "They're for you."

I laughed. "Girl, please."

"No, seriously," she said. "Somebody dropped them off and said, 'Give these to the girl on door.'"

Me? The girl on door?

I looked around like a camera crew was about to jump out and yell surprise. But no one came. Everyone just kept grinning, asking if I liked my flowers, like they all knew some secret I wasn't in on.

I never figured out who sent them.

I know who didn't send them, though—this little boy who used to come in all the time, couldn't have been more than eleven or twelve. He had the confidence of a grown man, always flirting, calling me pretty. I told him, "Baby, I can't do nothin' for you except let you watch movies." And that's what I did. Slipped him old ticket stubs when nobody was looking. He'd come back the next day, trying to act like it was a coincidence.

Weird little moments. But they gave me joy. Gave me laughter when everything else felt too heavy. And Lord knows, I needed those.

Because when you've carried trauma for years, you start to forget what simple joy feels like. You don't realize how numb you've gone until something wakes you up— a laugh, a flower, a kid with too much charm for his age. Those little things matter. They remind you that you're still alive. That somewhere inside the ache and the silence, you still have the capacity to smile.

I didn't have family dropping by to check on me. Didn't have a best friend calling just to say they missed me. What I had were scraps of light—pockets of kindness tucked into a very dark quilt.

Those memories? They were mine. Nobody could take them from me. They weren't just stories—I held them like evidence. Evidence that I had mattered, that at some point, someone had thought of me. I wasn't always invisible. And even if it was just for a moment, it meant something. Those were the kinds of memories that helped me keep breathing when I didn't think I could.

Because underneath the sarcasm, the quick wit, the practiced side-eyes and stiff posture—I was worn out. Not tired from the day, but soul-tired. From pretending. From performing. From holding in a scream that had been sitting in the back of my throat for years. A scream nobody seemed to notice. Or maybe they noticed, but ignored.

But I wasn't ready to say it out loud yet. Not the real thing. Not the part that lived beneath everything else. That kind of truth isn't made for microphones. It's not meant to be shouted from a stage or tucked into a testimony for applause. Some pain lives quieter. Some pain waits to be shared in a room where two broken women recognize each other without judgment.

So, I let the silence speak for me. I let those strange, sweet moments carry more weight than they should have. I let God hold the words I couldn't say. And somehow, even that helped.

The truth was—I missed home more than I ever let on. One night, I picked up the phone and called my little sister. Her voice alone nearly knocked the wind out of me.

We didn't talk long. Just enough to exchange updates and tiptoe around the weight we both carried. But afterward, I sat in the dark, phone still in hand, and cried harder than I had in months.

I realized I didn't have to keep punishing myself by staying away. I was surviving in Houston, yes—but barely. I had an apartment and a pulse, but not much else. The truth was, I had family back home. Friends. Familiar streets. More resources. I could go back and try again. Not to live under my mama's roof. Not to slip into old habits. But to rebuild from a new place. A braver place.

Avoiding my city hadn't healed me. It had just kept me in a different kind of prison. I'd blamed the city for the pain, but the zip code wasn't the problem. What happened to me was never my fault. I had to stop living like it was.

Then one day, I made a decision. A hard one. I packed up what little I had left. I said goodbye to Houston—not with bitterness, and not because I had failed. I left with hope. Real, trembling hope. The kind you whisper to yourself because it feels too fragile to say out loud.

I told myself I'd go home, but not the way I left it. And I damn sure wasn't going back to my family's doorstep like some burden they had to carry. I wasn't that girl anymore.

No more retreating.

No more making myself smaller to keep the peace.

No more asking permission to be whole.

This time, I was going home with a new kind of fire. Not loud. But steady.

And that was the beginning of something I hadn't dared to imagine for a long, long time—

The real beginning of honest healing.

CHAPTER 8

The Voice in the Pew

"To forgive is to set a prisoner free and discover
the prisoner was you."
— Lewis B. Smedes

"I Need You Now"
– Smokie Norful

I never planned to move back. Coming home felt too close to everything I'd spent years trying to forget. But after Houston, after the shelters and the prayers and the heartbreak, I needed a reset. Not just physically, but emotionally. Spiritually. And surprisingly, I didn't end up at Mama's house. I couldn't. The sight of them, their unknowing eyes, their small talk and shallow questions— they didn't know the truth, and I didn't have the strength to give it to them. So I chose space. Solitude. Safety. I just needed space to breathe without the judgment.

I found an apartment not too far from downtown. Small. Cheap. But mine. It had a window that faced the sunrise and a heater that clanged when it kicked on. I found a job. Something decent. Clock in, clock out, nobody asked too many questions. I told myself this was progress. Because it was.

But even with a roof and a paycheck, there was a stirring in me I didn't quite recognize, this ache that wouldn't quit. It wasn't loud, but it was persistent. A whisper, a nudge, something divine. Almost like my soul was tapping me on the shoulder, asking, "What now?" I didn't have an answer, but I did feel this strange, tender hunger to be useful. Not for recognition, not even for healing— just... to help. Like maybe, in pouring into someone else's emptiness, I could keep from drowning in my own.

So, one afternoon, on my way back from the corner store, I *saw* a two-story brick building. I had to emphasize "saw" because I had seen it, I knew it was there, I just never gave it much thought. It looked like an old house. Curtains in the windows, a white door, a tiny mailbox rusted at the edges. Just a regular house—two blocks from my apartment. But that day, something about it caught my eye. Maybe it was the flicker of movement at the window. Or the sound of laughter that didn't sound like it came from TV.

Maybe it was the sign, barely legible from the sidewalk,

tucked behind overgrown hedges: *Haven House Women's Shelter*. I'd walked that same block a hundred times. Never saw it once. But that day it was like it just... appeared. Like God peeled back the leaves on purpose. And I heard this quiet voice in me say, *Go in*. I didn't even argue. I just crossed the street and walked up to the porch.

Inside, it smelled like vanilla detergent and something frying in a pan. A woman at the front desk—gray-haired, kind eyes, maybe in her sixties—looked up. "Can I help you?" she asked. I hesitated. Then said, "I don't know. I was wondering if y'all needed help. Like... volunteering?"

She blinked, then smiled. "Well, we always need help." She handed me a clipboard. "Start with your name."

The shelter was started in the early '80s, founded by a retired nurse and a social worker who turned their grief into something generative after both lost loved ones to domestic violence. Their mission was simple: to offer safety, dignity, and a soft place to land for women in crisis. No judgment. No sermons. Just shelter, support, and second chances. Over the years, it grew from one house to two, eventually converting old bedrooms into offices, closets into counseling nooks, and the garage into a laundry room that never slept.

The staff was small but mighty. Miss T, the house manager, ran the place like a tight ship with a soft heart. There was Carla, a volunteer therapist who worked pro bono every Thursday night. Miss Cheryl handled scheduling and was the kind of woman who always had extra mints in her pocket. Tanya ran the kitchen and made the best rice and gravy this side of the South. There was also Marisol, a case manager who remembered every woman's name and trauma without needing to write it down. And then there were the other volunteers—college students, retirees, and now, me.

I didn't have a social work degree. I wasn't a counselor. I told them I didn't have much, but they welcomed my interest and said I could assist with intake and laundry duty. Three nights a week, I showed up. Quiet at first. Unsure. But there was something about that house, that rhythm, that steadiness—it steadied me, too. It was quiet on the outside, but alive with purpose on the inside. A mosaic of stories. Survivors. Strugglers. Seekers.

And to my surprise, I liked it. The folding. The warm hum of the dryer. The rhythm of it all. The soft, perfumed steam rising from clean sheets. The ritual of fresh towels, the quiet lull of women speaking low behind doors, the soft shuffle of slippers against tile floors. It was healing work, even if no one called it that.

There's something sacred about folding someone else's

clothes. It's the intimacy of care without intrusion. And the laundry room—well, that became my sanctuary. Warm. Safe. Predictable. A place where things got clean. The warm hum of the dryer. The rhythm of it all. I found peace in the repetition. The sorting. The stacking. The way it made order out of chaos. The quiet conversations. The tired eyes and brave smiles. I saw myself in so many of them. Especially one girl. Barely twenty. Thin, jumpy, always wore long sleeves even when it was hot. She said her name was Kia. Something about her stayed with me. The way she wouldn't meet anyone's eyes for too long. The way she flinched when the buzzer went off on the washing machine.

Sometimes I'd pause between loads and read the notes pinned on the wall—anonymous quotes from residents, scripture clippings, even a child's crayon drawing that simply said "Thank you." I didn't realize it right away, but this small, steamy garage room had become a chapel of sorts. A place where grief softened its edges. Where you could whisper your sadness to a machine and come back in 45 minutes to find it transformed.

I quickly learned their patterns. I noticed who never slept well, who paced the halls, who sat outside and smoked with their heads tipped toward the stars like they were begging heaven for answers.

Over the next three months, the women started to smile

when they saw me. They'd leave little notes on top of their baskets. One wrote, "Thank you for treating me like I matter." Another drew a tiny heart beside her name. "Thank you, Miss Ruth." "God bless." "You got the good folding hands." I'd laugh and wave it off, but truth was, I cherished it. I wasn't better than them. I *was* them. Still am.

But even as healing was blooming on one side of town, old wounds were festering on the other.

One average, painful day, I ended up at my sister's house. She was gone—out somewhere—and I was alone. Her place had that narrow hallway layout: kitchen, bathroom, bedroom on the left; living room, bedrooms on the right. I was in the back bedroom when I heard it. The front door opened. A voice called her name.

His voice.

My eyes scanned for something, anything—and there it was: a silver Louisville Slugger leaning behind the door. I grabbed it. Got into stance like I was waiting for a fastball. If that door moved, I was ready to decimate whatever came through. My hands shook. My breath shallow.

The sound of his voice—just three rooms away—had catapulted me straight back to 1996. That February. That loft. That silence before the slam.

They call it a *trauma trigger*—something sensory that pulls you back without permission. For some people, it's a smell. A sound. A certain type of touch. For me, it was *him*. His voice, still slow and sticky, like syrup over something rotten. My brain didn't care that I was older now, stronger, standing in my sister's bedroom and not in that quiet vacant cage. My brain just registered: **danger**.

That's how PTSD works. The body keeps score. The amygdala—your fear center—lights up like fireworks. Your hippocampus, the part that should remind you, "You're safe now," short-circuits. Your cortisol floods, your hands tremble, and suddenly you're nineteen again, no matter how many years have passed.

I gripped the silver bat like it was an extension of my bones. My palms were slick with sweat. I didn't blink. I stood there, breath shallow, hearing him turn the knobs—bathroom, bedroom, guest room—getting closer. Each click of a doorknob sounded like the cock of a gun. My vision narrowed. Tunnel. Black at the edges. My knees locked. I couldn't move if I wanted to.

I felt anger and rage. I thought I might swing too soon. I thought I might swing too late.

Then came the front door again. A pause. Then a slam. Then tires peeling gravel.

He was gone.

But the echo of his voice stayed. Not just in my ears—but in my bloodstream. It was like my body remembered him before my mind did. Before I could name it, the muscles in my back had clenched so tight it felt like my spine might snap. My stomach churned. I couldn't breathe right. Couldn't think straight. The air turned thick, like trying to swallow honey through a straw.

Yes, he was gone. But he had already broken the lock on my nervous system.

I lowered the bat like it weighed a hundred pounds. My arms burned. My body felt heavy, like I'd been underwater for hours and just surfaced. You ever been in a swimming pool too long, and when you climb out, gravity hits different? Like the weight of your own body surprises you?

That. Five times over.

I made it back to the bed and folded forward, hands in my lap, head down, like a child saying grace. And then I cried. For fifteen minutes. Couldn't stop. Couldn't catch my breath. I cried for the girl in 1996 who no one came for. For the woman I still didn't know how to protect.

And when the sobs finally slowed, something sharper moved in.

Clarity.

I thought about my sister. Her child. What it would mean to strike back. I told myself he could live—for the sake of the boy. My nephew deserved better than blood on his hands.

But the other one?

The one who hurt me the most?

My own cousin?

The one who dragged me by the neck while my limbs went limp?

He had to go.

Because by the time *he* touched me, I was already gone. The first assault had hollowed me out. Carved a silence so deep into my chest, I forgot how it felt to scream. After that, I didn't flinch. I didn't cry. I didn't even fight. It's not that I didn't want to—it's that I couldn't. When you've already died inside, what's one more burial?

That's the part no one talks about.

When a girl is assaulted once, the world around her tilts. She doubts herself, her voice, her right to feel safe in her own skin. But when it happens *again*—especially so soon after—the tilt becomes collapse. There's a term for it: "learned helplessness". It's what happens when you're harmed so deeply, so repeatedly, that your brain begins to believe resistance is useless. That your body doesn't belong to you. That you deserve nothing more than survival—and even that is negotiable.

The second time, I didn't even scream.

Not because I consented. But because something inside me had already been broken, and the pieces didn't make sound anymore.

It took me ten years to say the word rape.

Not because I didn't know what happened. But because I thought rape was just about the body. What I hadn't realized was that I'd been raped of far more than that. Trust. Joy. Laughter. Pride. Happiness. Love. All of it stripped from me in exchange for silence.

And silence, over time, becomes a second prison.

I didn't run to Houston because I had a dream. I ran

because I had nothing left. Not safety. Not worth. Not the belief that anyone would believe me—especially not about *family*. Because that's the other part. When it's someone who shares your blood, your shame multiplies. The betrayal is layered. Twisted. Rooted in the very soil that was supposed to grow you.

So when I sat on that bed, fifteen minutes after the voice of my first assailant cracked open a decade of pain, I didn't just cry for the first time.

I *remembered* for the first time.

And when I thought of my cousin, of his hands on me, of his laugh afterward like nothing sacred had just been stolen—I knew.

He had to go.

I made a plan.
I was going to buy a gun.
And I was going to use it.

Anyone who knew me knew I was terrified of guns—thanks to my grandmother, who kept one in her apron and could outshoot the police. But that day, I was past scared. Past shame. I was swimming in grief so thick it felt like gravity had tripled. I wasn't suicidal. I was homicidal.

And I was content with going to prison. I wasn't scared of prison. I was already serving a life sentence in my mind.

I had the day off. A rare Sunday with no shift, no obligations, just time. And I'd already made up my mind—he had to go. The decision sat quiet in my chest, like a final breath held before the plunge.

However, before anything else, I needed to go to church. One last time. Not for forgiveness—I wasn't there yet. Maybe to say goodbye. Maybe to ask God why He let it happen. Or if He even remembered me at all.

I got dressed slowly. Pulled on my favorite black pants— the ones that fit just right and made me feel like myself again. A loose blouse, soft earrings. No makeup, just lip balm. I didn't want to perform holiness. I just needed a pew.

I'd seen the church a few blocks over. Not one of those giant sanctuaries with LED screens and a Starbucks in the lobby. No. This was an old-school, Southern-rooted, all-Black church tucked between a fish market and a corner store. Brick building, chipped steps, and a marquee sign that still used plastic letters to list the sermon title.

As I walked up the sidewalk, the choir's warm-up notes

drifted out the open door. It smelled like pressed hair and peppermint. Someone held the door for me. "Come on in, baby," she said with a smile that reminded me of my Aunt Nettie.

The sanctuary was small. Pews polished with pledge. Ceiling fans spinning. Ushers in white gloves lining the back wall like soldiers. The deacons sat serious up front, heads bowed. The pastor adjusted his mic, flipping through a worn Bible with creased pages.

I slid into the back row. End seat. Always the end. The music started. It was familiar. Comforting. Routine. And for the first time in years, I felt something stir in me that wasn't rage.

I didn't know it yet, but God had already taken His seat beside me.

The service moved along like any Southern Black church on a Sunday morning. Choir in full voice, ushers nodding gently at latecomers, tambourines keeping time. The sanctuary was full of life—hollers of "Amen," hands lifted high, a cadence of call and response echoing between pulpit and pews. It felt like home. Familiar. Like something I used to know before the world fell apart.

But I wasn't really present. My body sat in that pew, but my mind was a battlefield.

I'd already made peace with what I was planning. Or at least, that's what I told myself. I'd asked God to forgive me in advance. I figured He might understand. After all, wasn't there justice in the Bible too? I wasn't some wild woman with a thirst for blood. I was tired. Tired of swallowing silence. Tired of nightmares. Tired of watching my own soul hemorrhage while the people who broke me walked around whole.

So I sat there, not in worship—but in war.

The choir swelled into a praise break. A woman danced down the aisle, waving her hands in surrender. Others followed, crying out with joy and release. The sanctuary rang with hallelujahs. But I sat stiff in my seat, arms crossed, staring past the pulpit. My jaw clenched. My fists curled in my lap.

Somewhere inside, I heard that small voice. *This isn't the way.* But I smothered it. I didn't want to hear right or wrong anymore. I knew murder was a sin. But I didn't care. Not right then. The one who hurt me the most—my own cousin—the one who dragged me like garbage and stripped me of everything? He didn't deserve air. Not after what he did.

The music rose. Feet stomped the floor in rhythm. A woman in front of me spoke in tongues. The pastor leaned into his mic, pacing, preparing to preach. I blinked, trying to stay grounded, but my vision wavered. My chest tightened. A prickle of heat ran up my neck. My face flushed. And then came the sting behind my eyes.

Tears. Not the slow, quiet kind. The kind that threatened to pour uncontrollably.

I closed my eyes tight, tried to hold it in.

But in that moment, something shifted in the air. The room didn't quiet, but something in me did.

I felt it—before I saw or heard a thing. A warmth beside me, so real it made my skin stand on edge. Like the presence of someone who knew me. All of me. And loved me still.

Then a hand. Not imagined. Not metaphor. An actual hand on my left shoulder. Gentle. Steady. And a voice— male, calm, and filled with something ancient and final.

"Vengeance is mine."

I opened my eyes.

No one was there.

Just noise and light and shouting and praise.

But I was soaked in tears, trembling from something I didn't understand.

A female usher bent beside me, rubbing my back. "He sho' can preach, huh?"

But the pastor hadn't said it.

No one had.

That voice—those words—they didn't come from man.

That was God.

And just like that, I never bought the gun.

I showed up to the shelter that night, different. Still shaken. Still healing. But something in me had settled. Not peace, not yet—but a strange kind of steadiness, like the moment before a storm breaks or right after a deep breath you didn't know you were holding.

The house was quiet. The kind of quiet that hums around you, not just through the air but in your bones. Most of the women had gone to bed. Their doors were closed, lights dimmed, the hallway still. I slipped into the laundry room, same as always, but everything felt different—like the walls knew. Like the machines were waiting.

Kia was already there, folding towels.

She didn't speak. Just kept her head down, stacking the white ones to the left, the colored ones to the right. I didn't say anything either. We just folded. For a long time.

Then she asked me softly, "Did you always know you wanted to help people?"

I don't know why that was the moment. Maybe because she asked it without expectation. Maybe because her voice sounded like my own at nineteen—small, unsure, tender from healing. But I felt it crack open something in me.

"No," I said.

And for the first time, I told someone the truth.

I told her about February 1996.

And I didn't flinch.

I started my period unexpectedly, and to my dismay, there was nothing available for protection. In a moment of desperation, my sister called her boyfriend for help. He arrived promptly, and I was able to purchase what I needed. However, instead of taking me home, he passed the familiar turn that would get us there, leaving me confused and uneasy. He continued driving until we reached a secluded little apartment nestled within a quiet plaza.

Upon arrival, I immediately inquired if there was a bathroom available. He confidently assured me there was, so I headed there with some relief. Unfortunately, upon entering, I was met with disappointment—it was missing all the essentials: no paper towels, no tissue, nothing at all. I found myself torn between the urgency to freshen up and the realization that I'd have to wait until I got home to do so properly. I decided to wait.

The place was peculiar; the left side featured walls leading up to a loft. On the right side, there were two small dens and a TV sitting room, and further back was a full-sized commercial kitchen that seemed out of place in such a setting.

Feeling increasingly uncomfortable, I went to stand by the front door, only to find it locked. Panic set in as he approached me, asking if I wanted him to take me home. I said yes, hoping for an end to this unsettling detour. Instead, he grabbed me with frightening force, dragged me up to the loft, and raped me.

I told her how I froze. How I felt myself leave my own body. How the walls blurred. How I stared at the ceiling fan and counted the rotations like maybe that would keep me alive.

I told her how I finally got home and cleaned up in silence. How I scrubbed until my skin burned, like maybe if I rubbed hard enough, I could erase it. Erase him. Erase me. I wanted to scream, but the house was quiet. I didn't want to wake anyone. I didn't want to be found crying, not like that.

And I thought about telling. I really did. A dozen times that night, I thought about shaking my sister awake and just saying it. Blurring the words into the dark between us: *He hurt me. I need help.* But then I imagined the questions. The face she'd make. The silence that would follow. Would she believe me? Would she still love me? Would she ask what I did to let it happen? And then what? Report it? Ruin her relationship? Tear our family apart?

I swallowed the words. And they never came back up. No police report. No one knew. Because I didn't tell.

The second time broke something deeper. About a month later, my cousin—someone I shared blood with—came at me like I wasn't even real. I didn't scream that time either. I didn't move. I just let it happen, like maybe I deserved it now. Like maybe I was already ruined. Already filthy. Already dead.

After that, I stopped trying to feel anything at all.

I told Kia how silence became my safest choice. My survival strategy. How the ache settled in like a tenant that wouldn't leave.

I told her about the red duffel bag I packed with one can of corn and five dollars. I told her about the Greyhound station. The stairwells. The police. How I didn't even know where I was going—just away. Away from shame. Away from memory. Away from them.

I told her I never got far enough.

I told her how I'd spent the next decade depressed, lost, angry, carrying shame that didn't belong to me. And I talked for nearly two hours. Everything I'd buried clawed its way out of me. The words poured. My voice cracked. My hands shook.

Kia cried through most of it. But she never looked away. And when I was finished, when the room finally fell quiet again, I realized I wasn't ashamed anymore—I was just tired.

And ready to heal.

She said, "Thank you for telling me. I thought I was the only one."

CHAPTER 9

Chasing Peace Around the World

"Not all those who wander are lost."
—J.R.R. Tolkien

"Stranger in Moscow"
– Michael Jackson

I didn't sleep much after talking to Kia.

Not because I was upset—but because something inside me had finally exhaled. I'd carried that story for so long, it had calcified. Hardened. Wrapped itself around the lining of my organs, my breath, my speech. And for the first time, I told it without apology. Without watering it down. Without wrapping it in politeness or disclaimers. I spoke from the raw middle of it. Kia had listened without flinching. In her tears, I found something like release.

That night, after I got home, I sat on the edge of my bed

for a long time. The silence around me felt different. It didn't press in on my chest like it usually did. It didn't feel like a trap. For the first time in years, it felt like space—room to stretch inside myself. I cried again—but they were different tears. Not from fear or guilt or sorrow, but from recognition. I saw myself clearly. I looked at the bruises on my past and realized they weren't proof of my weakness. They were proof I'd survived something no one should have had to endure. That girl in February 1996 had been so scared, so silenced, and yet—she had found a way to speak after all.

I hadn't realized how much that night in 1996 had been dictating the shape of my life. How that one hour had replayed itself—quietly and relentlessly—beneath my every decision, every silence, every time I told myself I was "fine." It had been my invisible compass, turning me away from closeness, from love, from believing I deserved softness. It had threaded itself into my sense of worth and whispered lies I accepted as truth: that I invited it, that I didn't fight hard enough, that I must have done something wrong. Shame has a way of dressing itself up in your own voice.

But telling Kia everything—*everything*—broke the mirror. Something shifted in my soul and I finally saw the truth.

I was a child. I was ambushed. I was terrified. And I

survived.

The shame didn't belong to me.

The blame was never mine.

Trauma that's not spoken aloud becomes a parasite. It feeds in secret. It latches to our nervous system, our immune response, our sleep cycles. It rewires the brain to anticipate danger, mistrust safety, and misinterpret love. For years, I mistook hypervigilance for intuition. Isolation for self-respect. Depression for my personality. But really, I was just carrying unspoken grief.

And what I now understand—what I hope someone else reading this might understand—is that healing doesn't require an immediate fix. It doesn't demand forgiveness or peace or moving on. But it *does* ask for truth. Even if whispered. Even if only spoken once. Because when trauma is witnessed in a safe space, its grip begins to loosen.

There's science behind it, too—though I didn't need science that night. I *felt* it. I *knew* it. But later, I read that narrating your traumatic experiences, especially in a nonjudgmental setting, actually helps the brain process and store the memory differently. The hippocampus, the part of the brain that contextualizes events, starts to regain control from the amygdala—the fear center. The trauma memory becomes integrated into your life story, instead of remaining a threat frozen in time.

That's what happened to me.

By telling Kia what happened, I reclaimed the timeline. I became the narrator. I stopped being just a scene in someone else's violence.

It was more than catharsis. It was liberation.

I felt lighter—not because the memory was gone, but because it was finally seen. Honored. Given language. There's something sacred about being known fully and still held. That's what Kia gave me. That's what I gave myself. And I realized: the guilt was never mine to carry. The silence wasn't protecting me—it was chaining me.

I'd been told, directly or indirectly, that speaking about "those things" made people uncomfortable. That good girls keep it to themselves. That family secrets should stay buried. But that night I unearthed it. Not for vengeance. Not for validation. But for *me*.

Because truth is oxygen and I was finally breathing again.

The next few weeks at the shelter, I kept showing up. Folding. Listening. Sitting still when needed. Kia stayed close, like a shadow, but one that made me feel less alone.

One night, she told me more about her own story—how she'd lived with an older man for more than three years. He was the kind that looked charming in public but snapped the moment the door closed behind them. Controlling. Manipulative. Violent. The kind of man who told you no one else would ever want you. Who tracked her every move and told her what to wear. Who slapped her across the mouth when she looked "too confident."

But that wasn't where her story started.

Kia said she was born addicted to crack. Her mother had been lost in the late '80s—another name in the long, quiet funeral line of the drug epidemic. She said the nurses didn't expect her to live more than a few days, but she did. Nobody came to get her. No system caught her. She just sort of... drifted. A distant aunt took her in first, then an uncle, then cousins, then back again. No one kept her long. Some didn't feed her. One kept her locked in a room during the day. She didn't remember hugs. Only shouting. Only hunger.

School saved her.

She said after seeing other kids outside the window, she started begging to go at five years old, just to escape the house. Her cousin eventually got her enrolled. Even when she was dirty. Even when she smelled like mildew or had holes in her shoes, she sat up straight and raised her hand.

She found a rhythm in the classroom—structure, peace, a reason to hope. Teachers noticed her. One used to keep peanut butter crackers in a drawer just for her. Another let her borrow socks. She was poor, yes—but she was brilliant. And she knew it.

That's what made the next part so cruel.

At thirteen, she said a man started showing up at her bus stop. At first, he just made small talk. Then he brought her candy. New socks. Compliments. "You're so grown for your age." "You got an old soul." "You're smarter than the rest of them." She said she knew it was wrong—some part of her always knew—but it felt like attention. Like warmth. Like safety dressed in danger's clothing.

By the time anyone noticed she wasn't coming to school anymore, it was too late. He had her. She said it didn't feel like kidnapping, but it was. He wrapped his rules around her like rope. First her friends. Then her routines. Then her meals. Then her sleep. Then her name. He started calling her by another name—"baby," or "mine"—until she almost forgot who Kia was.

But even inside that nightmare, her mind kept working. She read things he left out—old mail, flyers, used bus tickets. She memorized maps on takeout menus. She tucked pieces of herself into the corners of her brain, like a squirrel storing scraps for winter. And one night, when he left for a graveyard shift, she ran.

Barefoot. No plan. Just a backpack with three changes of clothes and a ten-dollar bill she found in an old pair of his jeans.

"I thought I was gonna die," she whispered, staring at her folded towel. "But something told me I was already dead if I stayed."

I knew that feeling.

Sometimes you don't leave because you're brave. You leave because you've already disappeared inside yourself, and you want to see if any part of you is still alive.

That's what Kia did. She didn't just escape him.

She chose herself.

And no matter what she thought she lost in the process, she won something sacred:

Her freedom. Her voice. Her future.

After hearing her story, I walked home with a strange

ache in my chest. Not sadness—something else. Almost like my soul was tapping me on the shoulder, asking, "What now?" I didn't have an answer, but I did feel this strange, tender hunger to be useful. To live beyond what had happened to me. To find joy somewhere in the world and touch it with my own hands.

And I started dreaming about leaving. Not to run, but to go. To experience beauty. Distance. Silence. Somewhere far enough that even my pain had to quiet down.

That's when I booked my first trip to Africa.

It didn't happen overnight. But once the seed was planted, it refused to die. I would find myself flipping through travel magazines at the library, running my fingers over glossy pages like they held secrets. Nigeria. Tanzania. Morocco. Namibia. I would catch foreign films on PBS and sit there, heart thudding in my chest, watching women walk through sunlit markets, brightly colored cloths fluttering around them like joy made visible. I wasn't jealous—I was captivated.

Growing up, my parents used to take us on summer trips. Not the beach-and-back kind, either. I'm talking full-on family vacations with itineraries, too much luggage, and hotel reservations booked months in advance. I'd been to the Statue of Liberty. Seen Mount Rushmore. Eaten real Chicago deep dish. Stared out over the Pacific Ocean while holding my daddy's hand. Travel wasn't a foreign concept to me. But luxury was. Freedom was. After 1996, I told myself those things weren't for girls like me anymore.

And yet... what if they were?

After talking to Kia, something inside me softened. For years, I'd built a life around low expectations. I didn't dare hope for anything extravagant—just survival. But trauma does that. It rewires your brain to protect itself. It's that "learned helplessness" again—the belief that no matter what you do, nothing will change. It's a mindset that numbs your imagination. But something about telling my story—actually narrating it in my own voice—began to undo that lie. I'd survived. I was still here. That meant something.

And if I could speak the truth about the worst day of my life, then maybe—just maybe—I could also speak possibility into my future.

I remember lying in bed that night, staring at the ceiling, imagining myself in a completely different time zone. I didn't know how much a passport cost. Didn't know which airline flew where. But for the first time in a very long time, I didn't shut the thought down. I let it grow. I whispered to myself, "What if?" And I didn't cringe when I said it.

I started small. A budget. A goal. I skipped takeout. Worked extra shifts. Took on cleaning work on Saturdays. I was exhausted, but it felt like I was building something. Every dollar was a brick in the road to somewhere else. Somewhere sacred. Somewhere safe.

And when I finally booked that ticket to Africa—one-way, no clue what I'd find—I didn't feel afraid.

I felt free.

I didn't just take trips. I *traveled* my depression away.

The first time I went to Africa, it felt like I had found a door in my soul I didn't know existed—and once I stepped through, I couldn't close it again. That trip didn't fix everything, but it gave me room to breathe, and that alone was holy. After years of suffocating in silence, shame, and four heavy walls that held too many memories, I finally exhaled in a land that had never heard my story—and still welcomed me.

Africa felt ancient in a way that cradled my spirit. The ground was red. The air, thick with sun and woodsmoke. And the people? Joyful. Resilient. It was as if God pressed His thumb into that soil and left the print of endurance. There was a slowness to life there, but not laziness—just reverence. A respect for time, for rhythm, for presence. I didn't even need to speak to feel understood. Just being *there* felt like medicine.

I wasn't rich. Not even close. But once I tasted that kind of freedom, I worked like hell to taste it again. I took every shift I could get. Nights. Weekends. Holidays. I'd been working security—a job that gave me exactly what I needed: space to think and no one asking questions. When the building emptied and the fluorescent lights buzzed overhead, I could just *be*. No mask. No pretense. Just me, watching the clock, dreaming about another plane ride.

My supervisor knew I was dependable, and that worked to my advantage. He hated being called in when folks didn't show up, so we made a quiet deal—he'd pick me up, bring me food, and I'd cover the shift. Overtime became my lifeline. That extra pay wasn't for bills—it was for my soul. For the moments I'd tuck away in a passport. I worked to escape. Not from life—but toward something better.

Africa cracked something open in me. But Japan? Japan became my *snuggery*. My safe place. My quiet miracle.

That country was... perfection. A harmony of discipline and beauty, modern and sacred. The kind of place where even chaos stands in line. My first day there, I swore I could write a whole book just standing on the corner. The order, the politeness, the kindness built into the culture—it felt like what I always imagined peace could look like.

I kept going back to Japan. Something about it called to me. Maybe it was the orderliness, the reverence for beauty, or the quiet beneath the chaos. I'd land, breathe in the air, and feel like I'd stepped into a world that had been touched directly by God's paintbrush.

Still, no matter how stunning the cherry blossoms or how futuristic the skyline, I couldn't shake the numbness. It was like seeing a dull rainbow—beauty was present, but I couldn't feel its magic. I was there, but not *in* it.

But that didn't mean I couldn't laugh.

On my third trip, I met up with a group of folks from the States—two men and a woman who taught English. We piled into one of their cars, which completely tripped me out. If you don't know, Japanese cars are flipped—driver's seat is on our passenger side. So when my friend kept asking if I was driving, I thought he'd lost his mind. Took me five whole minutes before I realized *he* was on the "right" side for Japan, and *I* looked like the designated driver.

We laughed hard at that. But nothing, *nothing*, prepared me for the taco incident.

We're driving, and I see this big sign: **TACOS**. I light up and say, "Ooooh, let's get some tacos! That'd be wild—eating a taco in Japan!"

They all burst into laughter. I mean, uncontrollable, belly-holding laughter. I'm confused, like, what's so funny?

Finally—**finally**—someone wipes their eyes and goes, "Taco means *octopus* in Japanese."

Let me tell you something: I did *not* eat the tacos.

Although... I did eat squid once. Thought it was spaghetti. Different story.

Later, at the guy's apartment—tiny little space, but enough—I ended up stuck in his bathroom for two hours. Think airplane-sized. I was trying to leave, but the door wouldn't open. I touched every wall, every button, and nothing. I just sat there. Eventually, I randomly pressed something, and the door slid open like magic. Of course I told him what happened. And of course he's *still* laughing about it—twenty-plus years later. Let it go, fam.

And the bathrooms! Lawd, the bathrooms.

We went to a traditional restaurant—tea came with everything, of course. I had to go, so the woman in our group pointed to the restroom. I came back confused.

"That's the *men's* bathroom," I said.

They fell out laughing again. Turns out, it was the women's. But instead of stalls, it was just a hole in the floor with a handle. No tutorial, no walkthrough, just floor-level plumbing. She thought it was *hilarious* watching me try to figure it out.

That's when she redeemed herself and said, "My apartment is next door. It has an American toilet."

I'd never been so happy to pee in my life.

But the real kicker came on my last day, in the airport bathroom. Tea, again. I sit, do my business, and go to flush. Or so I thought.

I hit the wrong button.

Next thing I know, jets of water shoot straight up my ass like a power wash. I yelped. Then came the air dryer—whoosh! More buttons, more panic, until I locked myself in again. I was stuck in this high-tech bidet box with no way out and no Kanji knowledge to save me.

Ten minutes later, I hear someone speaking English. "HEY!" I yelled. "Can you help me?"

She came over, and in the most casual tone said, "Oh,

there's a little button on the side. Just press that."

I barely made my flight. And I was *this close* to never using a public bathroom again.

But I can't lie: I miss it. The strawberry sandwiches—bread, whipped cream, and fresh strawberries—tasted like joy. My friend brought me one. I thought it would be disgusting, but it was like those yellow snack cakes with strawberry filling. Better, even.

Everything about that season was unfamiliar, unexpected, and a little messy. But I was learning how to laugh again. To move through the world with awe. Even when it made no sense.

Even when I got stuck in the bathroom—twice.

A beautiful chapter in my chaos, yet depression doesn't care where you go. I cried in Tokyo the same way I cried in Texas. I sat in hotel rooms staring at rice paper walls, numb. The beauty outside didn't always match the storm inside. But I kept going back. Four times, in fact. Something inside me just needed to be there. I remember how abrupt the third trip was. I was sitting at home, crying into a coat sleeve, thinking maybe I'd disappear right there on the couch. But then I got a call—my $2,000 check had come in. Just enough to cover one more flight. I booked the ticket through swollen eyes. Each visit was a search. Not for answers, but for breath. For stillness. For proof that the world still held things untouched by my pain.

That's the thing about travel—it doesn't erase the ache. But it gives you *distance* from it. It's a chance to step out of the heavy memories and watch yourself from a few thousand miles away. To remember that you are not just what happened to you.

Africa and Japan—so different they might as well exist on opposite ends of time. One looks like it just began; the other like it's already touched the future. But both of them? Both reminded me that God exists. That He's bigger than the pain I buried. That He whispers through acacia trees *and* bullet trains.

Sometimes I think about how many people never leave their zip code. Not because they don't want to, but because something inside them said, *You can't.* I lived with that lie for too long. But now? I knew better. Every trip was a rebellion. A reminder that I still had some say in how my story ended.

I didn't travel to escape life. I traveled to feel it. To remember that I had lungs. That I could laugh at something unfamiliar. That I could be lost in a foreign city and still belong to myself.

Each departure was a declaration: *I'm still here.* Each return, a quiet promise: *I'm not done yet.*

CHAPTER 10

The Day I Could Breathe Again

"I will not die an unlived life."
— Dawna Markova

"Pretty Wings"
— Maxwell

There comes a point when the numbness starts to rot.

You don't even notice it at first. Numbness feels like a gift in the beginning—like a warm coat in winter. A way to survive. A way to keep moving when your body remembers too much and your mind begs to forget. But after a while, it stops preserving you and starts consuming you.

That point came for me after years of crying in secret. Years of smiling with my mouth while my eyes stayed dull. Years of doing the robot shuffle through life, clocking in, clocking out, folding towels, paying bills, pretending to function. I became a master of routine, of silence, of managing other people's needs while mine withered from neglect. I wasn't "living" so much as I was floating just above the floor, untethered and unseen.

I had lived in that fog so long, I forgot what clear air smelled like. What it felt like to breathe without pain. Without fear. Without bracing myself for the next disappointment, the next trigger, the next moment of invisible collapse.

I didn't realize it was trauma. I didn't use that word. Back then, I just thought I was... broken. Hard to please. Angry for no reason. I thought I was bad at relationships. I chalked up my mistrust to being "realistic," my low standards to being humble, and my hypersensitivity to just "being dramatic." I didn't know I was still bleeding internally. I didn't know unprocessed trauma has a sneaky way of dressing up as shame. Of convincing you you're the problem, that you're just too much—or not enough—for anyone to ever really love.

But I didn't want to die like that.

I remember the moment it hit me—quiet, like a whisper in the middle of a loud world: *I don't want to leave this Earth sad.*

No matter what had been done to me—no matter what had been stolen—I wanted more. I needed more. I had to do whatever it took to get my joy back. I wanted to laugh without it catching in my throat. I wanted to look at the sky and see color again. I wanted to wake up and not dread it.

But first—I had to take the heaviest step of all.

I had to forgive them.

Now, let me tell you something—I did not go quietly. Baby, I fought that thing like a prizefighter with something to prove. I wrestled with the Lord like Jacob in a hoodie, barefoot in my living room at 2 a.m., flinging tears and curses and gospel music into the void. I begged Him for a different assignment. "God, please, can't I just rescue a cat from a tree instead? I hate heights... and I'm not even a cat person! I like goldfish!"

But He wasn't having it. God doesn't negotiate.

Every prayer I sent up, I got the same answer back like a voicemail stuck on repeat: **FORGIVE THEM.**

At first, I thought I could fake it. You know, do the performative "I'm healed" thing. I'd say the words, clap my hands, throw in a few Bible verses on social media. But inside I was still bitter. Still hurting. Still hoping they'd suffer for what they did.

That wasn't real forgiveness. That was the cheap kind—the kind you post about but don't actually live. The kind that looks good on paper but still poisons your soul.

I thought if I kept wearing my emotional mask long enough, it would eventually become my real face. That sucker was heavy. It came on and off like contact lenses. Except I wear glasses. So I was just walking around blurry and broken.

Still, I wasn't ready.

Not really.

Years passed. I kept waiting for the healing to come. Kept asking why I wasn't whole yet. Why I wasn't happy. Why the pain still hummed like static beneath the surface. I did everything right—went to work, showed up for people, tried to keep myself "busy" so I wouldn't have time to feel.

But that's the thing about wounds—you can't outwork them. You have to face them.

It wasn't until I met Kia that something finally shifted. The night I told her what really happened—the night I let those words out of my mouth for the first time, raw and unfiltered—something cracked open. It didn't erase the past. It didn't magically heal the pain. But it did something powerful: it gave me *options.*

Like a video game when you level up and suddenly you've got new tools, new weapons, new pathways to choose from. That's what speaking out gave me. It didn't close the loop. It opened it.

I started traveling not long after that. Not to run, but to expand. To experience something bigger than the life I had confined myself to. Beauty. Distance. Silence. I stood on foreign soil and felt my soul stretch a little wider. But even then—even with my passport stamped and my camera full of memories—I still hadn't unlocked the ultimate chamber of peace.

By 2010, I had pieced together something that resembled a life. I had a steady job that I actually enjoyed—quiet, consistent, mine. I wasn't clocking in every day trying to impress anybody. I was just doing the work, holding down my own. I had my own place, too. No more sleeping in stairwells or laundromats. No more fear that someone might tell me to move along. That space was small, but it was safe. And for a girl who once had nowhere to land, safety felt like wealth.

I was also starting to build relationships again—real ones. Not those trauma-bonded, half-hearted connections I used to cling to just to feel less alone. These new bonds were built on honesty, laughter, shared vulnerability. Women who saw me, not just my survival story. Friends who didn't need the edited version of my past. I was learning how to show up without flinching.

And I was learning what it meant to live without guilt.

But still… something was missing.

It was like living in a beautiful house with one locked room. Everything on the outside looked fine, even better than fine. But I couldn't shake the feeling that something sacred was still being held hostage inside me. I'd gotten so good at pretending I was okay that I'd forgotten what true peace even felt like. And deep down, I knew—if I wanted to experience real joy, I had to stop running from my faith.

I had to stop running from myself.

I'd been carrying a gospel in my pocket for years but treating it like it wasn't meant for me. I knew all the scriptures. I quoted them. Taught them. Shared them. But I wasn't *living* them. Not fully. Because the one thing God kept asking me to do was the one thing I refused to even consider.

Forgive them.

I thought I could bypass it. Take the scenic route. Do all the other healing work and leave that one part undone. But forgiveness isn't optional when you're seeking freedom. And the longer I avoided it, the heavier it became. Like dragging a rusted anchor through a river and calling it "progress."

It wasn't until I stood still—really stood still—that I faced the truth.

I was ready to change. I was ready to let go of the guilt that wasn't mine, the expectations I could never meet, the shame I didn't earn, the emotional laziness masquerading as numbness. I was ready to let go of that hollow place inside me that kept whispering *you're not enough*.

And it started with forgiveness.

God had given me the freedom to do it years ago. But I was stubborn. I wanted justice on my terms, healing without sacrifice. I didn't realize until 2011 that forgiveness wasn't for them. It was for *me*.

Forgiveness doesn't let the other person off the hook—it lets *you* off the leash.

It unclenches your fists.

It gives your soul back its breath.

It makes space for joy to come home.

That's when it finally hit me—I don't work for God like He's my employee. We work for *Him*.

And He wasn't on my timeline. I was on His.

So I did a deep dive into myself. No filter. No pretense. Just me and the truth, bare and brutal. I asked myself: What's more important—being right, or being free?

And when I finally let go—*really* let go—something happened.

Not in some grand hallelujah moment. But slowly, like breath returning after suffocation. Like light filtering in after a long night. Over time, I began to notice things in my spirit that had *never* been there before.

I stopped taking offense to every little thing.

That may not sound like much, but for me, it was revolutionary. For years, I walked around waiting to be wounded—reading every word, every side-eye, every silence as a personal attack. I was so used to being hurt that I carried my armor everywhere. I didn't know how to hear a question without thinking it was criticism.

Couldn't receive advice without assuming it was judgment. Even compliments made me suspicious. If someone said I was strong, I'd silently wonder what weakness they were trying to cover up. If someone said I looked nice, I'd brace myself for the "but."

But that started to fade.

It was subtle at first. Someone would say something that normally would've sent me into a spiral—and I'd pause, take a breath... and let it go. Not because I was pretending. But because it didn't sting anymore. Their words didn't stick. The hooks didn't catch. I realized the healing had worked its way down to my *identity*. I no longer saw myself as fragile. I didn't need to prove anything. I didn't need to defend every breath I took. And that freedom—Lord, that freedom—it softened me.

And with that softness came *space*.

Space to help. Space to serve. Space to look someone in the eye and say, "I've been through it too, but look at me—I made it." I wasn't ashamed of my assault anymore. I didn't feel like a walking secret. I wasn't hiding behind euphemisms and half-truths. I could tell the truth out loud without crumbling.

And something beautiful happened when I started telling it.

People started healing just from hearing it.

Women would pull me aside, whispering things they'd never said out loud before. Young girls would cry in my arms, releasing what they'd been holding. Survivors would lean in and ask, "How did you do it? How did you move forward?" And I'd tell them the only truth I know:

"I didn't. *God* did."

Because He doesn't ask us to be perfect. He doesn't ask us to have all the right words or feel the right feelings. All He asks is that we lean. That we trust Him enough to show up in our own lives—even if we're shaking. Even if we don't know what comes next. Even if we're still bleeding.

God will carry you through it, but only if you let Him lead.

And I didn't, not at first. I thought I could write my own blueprint. I thought I could outsmart the pain and shortcut the process. But all that did was prolong the ache.

It wasn't until I went *His* way that I found peace.

True peace.

It was 2011. I remember waking up one morning and feeling... strange. Off, but in the best way. The sky looked bluer. The grass greener. I could smell the blades. *Smell them.* I could hear birds like the world had been remastered in surround sound.

I felt still. I felt light. I felt… **Joy.**

Not the Instagram-filter joy. Not the "I'm blessed and highly favored" church smile.

Real, God-given, soul-thawing, spine-tingling joy.

I cried. And cried. And cried.
But this time, the tears didn't taste like grief.
They tasted like release.

That was the morning my healing got real.

That was the morning forgiveness bloomed in my chest like spring.

That was the morning I felt the hand of God resting gently on my shoulder, saying, *"You did it. Now let Me show you what peace feels like."*

It's been fourteen years since that morning.

And I have never—*never*—been happier.

If it had not been for the Lord on my side... Tell me—

where would I be?

Oh, Lord...
Where would I be?

EPILOGUE

The Purpose Was Bigger Than Me

"I am still here, breathing, living, loving, fighting."
—Unknown

"Completely Yes"
- Sandra Crouch

What follows is not another chapter, but a final offering—my way of saying: I'm still here. I made it. And you can too.

There are some moments in life when you realize the storm wasn't meant to drown you—it was meant to water the seeds buried in you. That's what 2023 taught me.

I had just gotten used to the taste of joy again. That Chapter 10 kind of joy—the slow, deep-breath joy. I was working. I was stable. I was volunteering three nights a week at the shelter, folding laundry and wiping down cots

141

like it was sacred work. Because it *was*. And even though the nights still got quiet sometimes—and quiet still got lonely sometimes—I wasn't afraid of the silence anymore. I had found peace.

But then… the lump.

The appointment. The scan. The call.

"Stage 0 to 1. It's early."

That's what they said. Early. Like it was supposed to make it easier. Like catching cancer before it took root was the same as not having cancer at all.

But cancer is cancer. And when you've spent your life surviving one fight just to wake up in another, it's hard not to feel betrayed by your own body.

I could feel it coming—*that old weight*. Depression started creeping in around the edges of my thoughts like mildew. It wanted to drag me back to that place. The dark. The numb. The "just go through the motions" place I'd spent years clawing my way out of.

But this time… I didn't let it.

No ma'am. Not again. Not this girl.

I made a decision. Right then, in the middle of my living room, wearing my house dress and slippers with a hole in the toe. I told God, "I will not spiral. I will not disappear. I will *not* go backward."

He didn't say anything in that moment—He didn't have to. We had been through enough together. I knew He heard me.

And then something strange happened. A delivery driver pulled up to my gate. One of those third-party folks— worked for MALWART or whatever they call it now. Young guy. Wore a beanie even though it was 75 degrees. Talked soft. Said he noticed my hair. I laughed. It was a mess. I hadn't washed it in weeks, hadn't had the strength. But he wasn't trying to be rude.

He said, "I do hair. Mind if I read yours?"

I blinked. "Read it?"

"Yeah," he grinned. "Hair tells stories."

Now, listen. I've heard a lot of things in my life—but never that one. Still, something in his tone… it was warm. He wasn't flirting. He wasn't selling. He was seeing me.

He gave me his card. I gave him my number.

We scheduled something three months later—when I could afford to have my head touched again.

The wash, honey…

That shampoo was holy.

I don't know what happened. I don't know *how* it happened. But as Lamar's hands moved through my scalp, I felt the weight of every medical appointment, every needle prick, every "you'll need to follow up"—start to melt away. It was like the water carried my worries right down the drain. I could've cried right there in that chair. And maybe I did. I don't know. I just remember feeling… covered.

That's when the idea came to me.

If I could feel this—this calm, this ease—why couldn't other women? Why couldn't a moment like that, one simple act of care, help someone else believe they were still worthy of softness?

So I started *The 306 Project*.

Three-oh-six. March 6th was the date of my first appointment. The charge was $35 for the service, but I always pay $36 for myself and the extra dollar goes towards the project.

That's all some women need—a moment.
A break from the fight. A little dignity.

So I made it a mission. I told Lamar what I wanted to do,
and he was in. No hesitation. I started paying for other
women to get a silk press, or a mani-pedi, or whatever
small thing helped them feel human again. The only
"requirement" was that they be in a shelter, starting over,
or simply broken and trying.

Some I found. Some he found. Some God sent.

Seven or eight women so far. That's all I could afford.
But each one smiled different afterward. Stood taller.
Walked out the salon with a head held higher. Not
because of the style—but because someone believed they
were worth seeing.

Even when my bank account got low, I kept going.
Sometimes, when I felt the sadness creeping again, I'd go
get my hair done too. That chair became holy ground for
me. A place of reset.

And as my outer body was being nurtured, something
inside me was being reborn.

I started cleaning my kitchen more. Playing gospel music

before the sun came up. I let go of the idea that I had to be "healed" in full before I helped anybody else. I stopped hiding behind shame. Stopped covering my smile with my hand because of my yellowed teeth. One day, I scraped up $135 and went to a dental school to have them whitened. They weren't perfect after, but they were *better*—and that was enough. That was hope.

See, people think healing is this glamorous thing. But sometimes healing just looks like brushing your teeth. Making your bed. Calling someone back.
Saying, "I'm sorry."
Saying, "I forgive you."
Saying, "I'm still here."

I gave God my broken soul—and He gave me a purpose.

This was never a story about being raped.

That was just the storm that tried to take me out. But it didn't.

This is a story about **faith**. About how forgiveness didn't kill me—it *saved* me. And I don't say that lightly.

Forgiving was the hardest and easiest thing I've ever done in my life. Both things. At the same time. Like peeling skin off a sunburn and watching new life grow underneath. It took *everything* out of me to do it. But when it was done, I realized—it was never about them.

It was about me.

Forgiveness is freedom for the one who gives it.

And honey, I am *free*.

I don't take offense like I used to. I don't bristle every time someone has a tone. I don't think every comment is an attack or a judgment. I walk in rooms now with my head up, knowing I belong. Knowing my story is not a burden—it's a blueprint.

I reach out more. I call women I haven't spoken to in years. I tell them the truth—that healing is messy and hard, but it's worth it. That God doesn't ask us for perfection. Just surrender. That even when you've lost your way, He's still holding the map.

When I look at The 306 Project now, I see legacy. I see ministry.

I used to think ministry meant preaching or laying hands on someone at the altar.

Now I know ministry can be a silk press.

Ministry can be a warm hand on a cold shoulder. A $35 gift card. A gentle, "You're still worth it."

And that's what I live for now.

Every woman I help is a reminder that I didn't die in that trauma. I lived. I *live*.

I don't fear death anymore. Not because I'm unafraid, but because there is no hate in me. No bitterness. No anger left.

Just grace.
Just peace.
Just purpose.

I could recite Psalm 23 right here and now. Word for word. I know it like I know my own story.

"The Lord is my shepherd..." That's my relationship.

"I shall not want..." That's my supply.

"He maketh me to lie down in green pastures..." That's my rest.

And I rest now. Fully. Even in chaos. Even with bills due. Even with cancer scans still marked on the calendar. I rest because I know who holds me.

God isn't finished with me yet.

But even if He called me home today, I'd go knowing I loved well, forgave fully, and lived without regret.

If you remember anything I've written in these pages, let it be this:

The same God who made the storm made the rainbow.
The same God who made the thorn made the rose.
The same God who made the vulture made the peacock.
He can make beauty from pain.
He can make healing from horror.
He can make purpose from brokenness.

Even a Sequoia starts with a seed.

And baby... if He can do that with me?

He can do it with you, too.

The valley was dark, but the mountain is bright. The wounds were deep, but the healing is real. I gave Him my yes. Completely.

And that's when everything changed.

THE END. *(But also… the beginning.)*

Final Word: Psalm 23, Rewritten with Truth

The Lord is my Shepherd.
That's Relationship!

I shall not want.
That's Supply!

He maketh me to lie down in green pastures.
That's Rest!

He leadeth me beside the still waters.
That's Refreshment!

He restoreth my soul.
That's Healing!

He leadeth me in the paths of righteousness.
That's Guidance!

For His name's sake.
That's Purpose!

Yea, though I walk through the valley of the shadow of death.
That's Testing!

I will fear no evil.
That's Protection!

For Thou art with me.
That's Faithfulness!

Thy rod and Thy staff, they comfort me.
That's Discipline!

Thou preparest a table before me in the presence of mine enemies.
That's Hope!

Thou anointest my head with oil.
That's Consecration!

My cup runneth over.
That's Abundance!

Surely goodness and mercy shall follow me all the days of my life.
That's Blessing!

And I will dwell in the house of the Lord.
That's Security!

Forever.
That's Eternity!

Face it—God loves you.
What is most valuable is not *what* we have in our lives, but **who** we have in our lives.

Soundtrack: Songs That Carried Me Through

These are the songs that walked with me through the fire—through heartbreak, healing, faith, and forgiveness. Each one helped hold a piece of me together. Maybe they'll carry you, too.

1. **Deitrick Haddon** — *"A Sinner's Prayer"*
2. **Beyoncé** — *"He Still Loves Me"*
3. **Marvin Winans** — *"You Just Don't Wanna Know"*
4. **Maxwell** — *"Pretty Wings"*
5. **Joss Stone** — *"Right to Be Wrong"*
6. **Bobby Ross Avila** — *"Between a Rock & a Stone"*
7. **Yolanda Adams** — *"Open Up My Heart"*
8. **Yolanda Adams** — *"The Battle Is Not Yours"*
9. **Tamela Mann** — *"Take Me to the King"*
10. **Fleetwood Mac** — *"Landslide"*
11. **The Clark Sisters** — *"You Brought the Sunshine"*
12. **New Jersey Mass Choir** — *"Oh the Blood"*
13. **The Winans** — *"Tomorrow"*
14. **Patti LaBelle** — *"When You've Been Blessed"*
15. **Shirley Caesar** — *"No Charge"*
16. **Michael Jackson** — *"Stranger in Moscow"*
17. **Mary Mary** — *"Yesterday"*
18. **Smokie Norful** — *"I Need You"*
19. **Smokie Norful** — *"Still Say Thank You"*
20. **Rev. James Cleveland** — *"Remember Me"*
21. **Vickie Winans** — *"Safe in His Arms"*
22. **Sandra Crouch** — *"Completely Yes"*